"Do you think Daddy's ever going to find us a mommy?"

Justin sighed. "He didn't even like that picture." His voice lowered to a whisper. "Was she really naked?"

"Naw," Gareth assured his twin. "She was wearing a swimsuit or something. But girls sure are different from us."

"If Daddy doesn't like looking at girls, how will he ever find us a mommy?"

With the wisdom of a five-year-old, Gareth explained, "He's trying to find a housekeeper and nanny instead."

"But Moss said no one answered that ad. But when Moss changed the ad to one for a wife, then 'every bloomin' female in the county wrote a letter.'" He mimicked the man's drawl.

"But if Daddy doesn't like 'em, it doesn't matter. We need someone to help us, someone who'll give us what we ask for."

"Hey!" Justin beamed, excitement filling his voice. "We can ask Santa…. He'll give us a mama for Christmas!"

Dear Reader,

There's nothing more magical about Christmas than the faces of the children when they run downstairs to see what Santa has left them under the tree. For me, and for every parent, the smiles on my two sons' faces are presents enough! This month American Romance is bringing you all that excitement and more in our special "Christmas Is for Kids" promotion.

By popular demand "Christmas Is for Kids" is back—with four brand-new stories to warm your heart. Spend this holiday season with some of the most precious—and precocious—kids, who team up with Santa to play matchmaker for their unsuspecting moms and dads.

Don't miss any of the "Christmas Is for Kids" books this month!

From my family to yours, Merry Christmas!

Debra Matteucci
Senior Editor & Editorial Coordinator
Harlequin
300 E. 42nd St.
New York, NY 10017

Judy Christenberry

WANTED: CHRISTMAS MOMMY

Harlequin Books

TORONTO • NEW YORK • LONDON
AMSTERDAM • PARIS • SYDNEY • HAMBURG
STOCKHOLM • ATHENS • TOKYO • MILAN
MADRID • WARSAW • BUDAPEST • AUCKLAND

ISBN 0-373-16612-5

WANTED: CHRISTMAS MOMMY

Prologue

"Any luck?"

Doug Graybow had been scowling into his beer when one of his neighbors settled into the chair across from him. "Nope," he admitted. "I've been running the ad for three or four weeks now, and I haven't had a single applicant."

"What are you gonna do?" Ben Anderson asked.

"About what?" another neighbor, Will Jacks, asked as he joined them. They'd all just left the Ranchers' Association monthly meeting in the back room of the Riverside Café and, as was custom, were settling in for a few beers with their neighbors.

"Doug, here, has been advertising for a housekeeper to replace Agnes. She and Rocky retired to Arizona, you know."

"Oh, yeah, I heard that. And you haven't had any luck?" Will asked.

"Nope," Doug repeated, weariness in his tone as well as his posture.

"Man, those holy terrors of yours must be driving you crazy," Will said with a grin.

Doug didn't bother to defend his progeny. No one would believe him. The five-year-old twins had been bad enough with Agnes to corral them. Since she'd packed her bags and headed south, they'd been impossible.

Ben smacked his hand down on the table, startling both his companions. "Damn it, man, you're advertising for the wrong thing!"

"What are you talking about?" Doug wondered if his friend had already imbibed several beers before joining him.

"You should be advertising for a wife. That's what you need. Not a housekeeper. Housekeepers leave, but a wife will put up with anything if you cuddle her a little and buy her something pretty every once in a while."

Ben grinned as if he'd just made a major discovery, and Will nodded in agreement.

Doug frowned at him, irritation in his every bone. "First of all, if that's the way you're treating Meggy, I hope she throws you out on your ear. And I'm not about to advertise for a wife. Any woman desperate enough to answer that kind of ad wouldn't be the woman for me."

Besides, he'd tried marriage once. He wasn't sure he would ever be *that* desperate—in spite of the disasters his sons could create. He'd find a housekeeper somehow. Somewhere.

Unable to stand any more conversation on the subject, he stood, grabbed his cowboy hat and sheepskin jacket from the back of the chair, muttered a good-night and stalked out into the cold November air.

"Man, he's a touchy son of a gun tonight," Will protested.

"I bet it's those kids of his. Meggy has 'em in Sunday school and she comes home all worn-out. They need a mama real bad."

"Well, he oughta consider a ad. I heard tell of a man up in Wind River got a wife that way."

"He'd be more likely to find a woman that way than just waitin' for one to come along. Wyoming may have lots of things goin' for it, but available women isn't one of 'em."

"You're right about that," Will agreed. "Too bad we can't put in a ad for him. Once he met a few of those 'desperate' women, he might change his mind."

"Yeah, too bad—" Ben stopped and stared at his friend. "Why not? You got a piece of paper?"

Chapter One

"Damn!"

The five-year-old twins stared at each other before one whispered, "Ooh! Daddy said a bad word."

"I heard that." The deep voice sounded from above the desk.

"Well, you did," Justin asserted.

"Yeah, we heard you," his twin, Gareth, agreed.

They watched as their father sighed and ran his hand through blond hair only slightly darker than theirs. He looked down at them and muttered, "Sorry, guys, I shouldn't have said a bad word, but I'm a little upset."

"How come? We didn't even do anything today," Gareth protested.

"I know. It's not you. It's these blasted letters." He shoved at a pile of papers and envelopes and several fluttered to the floor.

The boys started gathering them up for their father when Gareth found a picture. "Wow! She don't hardly have any clothes on!"

Justin leaned over to see the picture, but their father snatched it from Gareth first.

"Give that to me! Uh, thanks for trying to help, boys,

but I, uh, need you to go play or watch TV or...or something."

There was a tone in his voice the boys had heard before. A tone that said their father had reached his limit.

"Yes, Daddy," they chorused, their angelic smiles matching the blond innocence on their faces. They tiptoed from the room, pausing only to look once more at their father's flushed face as he stared at yet another letter.

Once they were in the living room with the TV turned on, Justin said, "Do you think Daddy's going to find us a mommy?"

"I don't know. He doesn't seem too happy."

"He didn't even like that picture." He paused before asking his brother in a whisper, though no one could hear them, "Was she really naked?"

"Naw," Gareth assured him. "She was wearing a swimsuit or something. But girls sure are different from us." He glanced down at his flat, narrow chest with a frown.

"Yeah. Curly looks at pictures like that sometimes," Justin added, naming one of their father's cowboys.

"Yeah."

Justin thought a littler longer, a mighty frown on his face. "If Daddy doesn't even like to look at pictures of girls, how will he find us a mommy?"

"He's trying to find someone to take care of us instead of a mommy. He said."

"I know. But no one answered that ad. I heard Moss and Curly talking," Justin explained. Moss, their father's foreman, was a great favorite with the twins. "They said Daddy didn't get no answer to his ad. But when Mrs. Meggy's husband changed the ad to one for a wife, then 'every bloomin' female in the country wrote a letter,'" Justin finished triumphantly, having produced a semblance of Moss's drawl as he quoted him.

"But if Daddy doesn't like 'em, it doesn't matter," Gareth reasoned.

"Yeah." Justin slumped against the back of the sofa. "But *I* want a mommy. Don't you?"

"Yeah. One who makes cookies...and tucks us in at night."

The two boys sat in silence, contemplating the idea of having a mother. They were a little fuzzy on the details, but they knew they wanted one.

"But if Daddy won't pick one, how will we find a mommy?" Justin finally asked.

"We could send a letter to the paper, like Mrs. Meggy's husband did."

"We don't know how to write."

"Oh. Yeah."

"We need someone to help us," Justin said, frowning again. "Someone who will give us what we ask for."

"That sounds like Santa Claus," Gareth said before he straightened, excitement filling his voice. "Hey! We can ask Santa for a mommy for Christmas. She can be our present this year!"

THE INCESSANT RINGING of the phone had Doug muttering a few more of those forbidden words beneath his breath. He trudged down the hall and into the kitchen to grab the receiver.

"Yeah?"

"Doug Graybow? Ooh! You sound *hot!* Wait till you see just how hot I can be, too. We'll be perfect for each other."

"Look, if this is about the ad, it was a mistake."

"But, Dougie, I'm sure you'll be interested in what I have to offer. I'm 38-22-34, have long blond hair and—"

Doug interrupted the sultry voice. "Sorry, not interested." He slammed down the phone and started back to his office. That was the fifth call this evening, interrupting his paperwork. Fed up, he paused by the living room door. Sticking his head in, he said to his sons, "If the phone rings anymore, just tell them I'm busy and hang up. Okay?"

"You mean we get to answer the phone?" Gareth demanded, excited about the new responsibility.

"That's right. But do exactly like I tell you. If they ask to speak to me, tell them I'm busy and hang up."

"Okay," the twins chorused.

He turned away from his grinning sons, a little uneasy about what he'd done, but he couldn't take care of everything and continue to answer those ridiculous calls.

Life was screwy. Four weeks advertising for a housekeeper and not a single call or letter. One week of that stupid ad for a wife, and he was being driven crazy by the calls and, even worse, the letters. The picture Gareth had found was mild in comparison to some he'd received. He blushed just thinking about them.

When he'd come in this evening, his answering machine had been full of suggestive messages, asking him to call. Most left their home numbers. One particularly sexy voice had suggested he call her at a motel in Dodge City, Kansas, so they could discuss fulfilling their mutual needs. Maybe she expected him to drive to meet her so they could "try out" married life.

He settled back in at his desk and, in disgust, swept the letters into the trash. He'd wasted enough time on such foolishness!

LESLIE HIBBETS SWITCHED the TV channel again. The tired, out-of-date motel room in Dodge City, Kansas, didn't offer much in the way of entertainment. But she couldn't leave unless she wanted to risk missing her return call.

Last night, she'd gone to the diner next door for a late meal, discouraged and unsure of her next move. She'd spent the past four years nursing her mother after an accident had killed her father and left her mother crippled. Six months ago her mother had died.

Feeling her life had been put on hold, albeit for a good reason, Leslie wanted to experience life, to find excitement. Instead, all she'd found was loneliness.

Eventually, she wanted to have a family, much like the life she'd experienced as a child. Her parents had provided a loving home for her, a home where she knew her parents loved each other as well as her. In the meantime, she wasn't quite sure what she was looking for.

While waiting for her food, she'd glanced at the weekly newspaper someone had left on the counter. Out of boredom, she'd turned to the want ads. The only one that caught her eye was for that of a housekeeper for a rancher with five-year-old twins.

If there was one thing she could do, it was keep house. She didn't know much about children, but she could cook. Of course, she had no intention of being tied down, she reminded herself. She was free now to discover the world.

A rueful laugh had escaped at such grandiose thoughts. All she'd discovered had been highways with traffic whizzing by and lonely motel rooms. She looked at the ad again. If she took something like this job, on a temporary basis, just until the children started school, it would give her time to figure out what she wanted to do. And she wouldn't feel so...so unconnected.

Money wasn't a problem, but she couldn't go forever without a job. Why not earn her keep while she was determining her future?

She'd decided to sleep on her decision. When she awoke this morning, she'd made the phone call to Mr. D. Graybow in Wyoming and gotten the answering machine. His gruff, sexy growl had startled her and she'd hung up. Before she lost her courage, she redialed the number and this time, she left a message, suggesting he call her to discuss fulfilling their mutual needs.

"There!" she'd exclaimed as she'd hung up. She'd sounded cool and professional—she hoped. Now all she had to do was wait for him to call.

By nine o'clock that evening, her patience was wearing thin. The least the man could do was return her call. Impatiently, she picked up the phone and dialed the number in the ad.

"Hello?"

She realized a child had answered the phone, probably one of the twins. "May I speak to Mr. Graybow, please?"

"He's busy."

Before she could respond, the line went dead. She held the receiver from her ear and stared at it as if it had insulted her.

Irritated, she dialed the number again. The same little voice answered and she hurriedly asked, "Mr. Graybow, please."

"He's busy." Again the line went dead.

With steely determination, she dialed again. "Don't hang up!" she immediately said when the child answered again. "I'm calling about the ad. Has Mr. Graybow hired anyone yet?"

There was no response to her question but she could hear hurried whispering in the background. "Hello?"

"No, he hasn't."

"Well, uh, if he won't interview me over the phone, should I come there? Is he only interviewing in person?"

More whispering.

"Can you bake cookies?"

Leslie smiled at the question. "Yes, I can bake cookies."

"Do you like little boys?"

"Yes, I believe I do." Not exactly a lie. She just hadn't been around little boys that much, except for her neighbor's grandchildren.

"Then you should come."

"I should come? When?"

"Now."

"But I can't get there until tomorrow. Shall I come tomorrow evening?" How strange to allow a five-year-old to conduct his business. Mr. D. Graybow certainly seemed in need of some help. She ignored the sudden memory of that husky voice on the answering machine.

"Yeah. Tomorrow night. Bye!" Again the conversation ended abruptly.

But this time she had an answer to her question. She was to go to Wyoming to interview for a temporary job as housekeeper.

Of course, it might all come to nothing, but she'd wanted adventure. She wasn't going to retreat at the first offer just because the future wasn't guaranteed.

Twenty-four hours later, her opinion changed. "You are crazy!" she told herself. Leslie gnawed on her bottom lip as she stared down the narrow, deserted road. When it got dark in Wyoming, it really got dark.

Back home in Kansas City, there always seemed to be another house, a store, something around the bend. People passing you on the road.

Out here, there was nothing. She hadn't seen another car in the past half hour. Glancing down at the piece of paper on the other seat, she wondered if she was lost. No, she hadn't passed another road like the one shown on the sketchy map the motel clerk had given her. After she'd gotten a room, she'd headed out to the Bar-G Ranch, as per the child's instructions last night.

She shuddered as a strong wind rocked the car and wet flakes of snow began spitting on her windshield. "Yes, you're absolutely crazy," she reaffirmed. Otherwise she wouldn't have taken a child's word that she should come. But at least she'd had a purpose to her drive today.

A break in the fence on her right that she could barely see in the dark had her easing off the gas pedal. Yes, there it was, just as the clerk had said. She flicked on her blinker and then laughed. Who cared if she signaled? She seemed to be the only driver for miles around.

Not that being alone bothered her. She'd spent a lot of time alone or with her mother for the past four years.

She drove over a cattle guard, but if she'd expected to find a ranch house nearby, she was disappointed. No habitation was within the range of her headlights.

With a sigh, she pressed back down on the gas pedal. She might as well get this over with. If this job didn't work out, she'd have to try to make a rational decision about her future. She couldn't continue to wander around.

Two miles later, she found D. Graybow's house, surrounded by several other buildings. There were lights burning, she noted with a sigh of relief. She guessed they really were expecting her.

She parked the car close to a long porch that ran the length of the house. Warily she climbed the steps and rapped on the door.

No one answered at first. She rapped again. This time she heard voices, children's voices, and then a deeper voice, accompanied by a heavy tread. She recognized that growl.

The door swung open and she stared at a handsome cowboy—tight jeans, boots and all. Of course, his shirt was wrinkled and had stains, his hair looked as if he'd just shoved one of his big hands through it and the scowl on his face was unwelcoming. But he was handsome.

"Mr. Graybow?"

"Yeah?"

Definitely unwelcoming.

"I've come about your ad."

HE COULDN'T BELIEVE IT. The letters had been bad enough. The letters and the pictures, he amended. He couldn't believe women would go so far to find a husband. Some of those things had been downright embarrassing. But to appear on his doorstep with no warning?

Something about the voice sparked a memory in him. The sexy voice on the answering machine wanting to discuss fulfilling their mutual needs! He'd had dreams about that voice.

"I realize it's late, but he said to come tonight," she went on, since he didn't speak. "And I just got here from Kansas."

"The ad was a mistake," he snapped. And one his idiotic friends would pay for when he got his hands on them.

"Oh."

The single syllable was full of disappointment. He looked at her, wondering why she would be so interested in marrying a stranger. It didn't make sense to him. She wasn't ugly. In fact, in his book she'd rate a second look with her wide blue eyes, chestnut hair pulled back in a braid and slender figure. *If* he were interested in marrying again, he hurriedly reminded himself.

A tug on his leg got his attention.

"Daddy?"

"Not now, Gareth," he muttered. Somehow it bothered him that his children meet a woman desperate enough to answer that crazy ad.

"But, Daddy—"

"I said not now!"

The woman was turning away from the door when Justin, Gareth's twin brother, called from the kitchen, "Hurry, it's getting bigger."

The woman stopped and stared at them, a puzzled frown on her face. He nodded at her and started closing the door, anxious to send her on her way. But a look in her eyes stopped him. She was staring in horror over his shoulder.

Uneasiness filled him as he turned to follow her gaze.

With good reason. Black smoke was trailing out the kitchen door.

Chapter Two

"Justin!" Doug yelled even as he charged down the hall. The appearance of his towheaded son at the door was a relief, but he didn't have time to appreciate it then.

Racing into the kitchen, he grabbed the handle of the skillet on the burner, the flames in it higher than the ones underneath. As he swung it to the sink, the searing iron of the skillet burned into his hand, and he let loose a bloodcurdling yell.

A slim hand reached around him and turned on the cold water, directing the flow into the skillet. The smoke tripled as cold met hot. Before he could think how to relieve the pain that was shooting through him, that same hand grabbed his and, redirecting the water to the other sink, put his palm under the flow of water.

"Don't move," she ordered.

Vaguely he was aware she'd extinguished the flames on the stove. But he didn't know where she went until she dumped a handful of ice cubes into the deepening water. But he wasn't going to complain. He was in agony.

"Aren't you supposed to use butter or something?" he asked, his voice gritty as he tried to hide his pain.

"No. That's the worst thing to use." She made another trip to the refrigerator for more ice.

He had forgotten his children until he heard a giggle and then watched as they dropped ice cubes into the water.

"We never made icewater in the sink before. Is Daddy gonna drink it?" Justin asked.

"No, he's not," the woman answered, smiling at the boy. "We're trying to stop his hand from burning."

"Like the skillet? Is he gonna have fire in his hand?" Gareth asked as he rose on tiptoe to peer over the side of the sink.

"No," she said again. "But his hand is going to hurt a lot."

Justin and Gareth frowned.

"Does it, Daddy?" Gareth finally asked.

"What?" Doug muttered, his mind intent on the woman's actions rather than his sons.

"Does it hurt really bad?"

"Yeah." His gaze met the woman's and he realized he owed her his thanks. "Uh, I appreciate your help."

A half smile and a shrug was her only response.

"How long do I have to keep my hand in the water?"

"You can take it out whenever you want, but it's best to keep it in until the burning stops." She had that sexy voice he remembered from the answering machine— soothing at the moment, warm.

"I'm gonna look pretty funny on a horse with a sink attached," he muttered.

Another smile. Suddenly he wondered if she ever laughed. If her blue eyes lit up and her lips— What was wrong with him? He didn't even know this woman.

"I think a half hour will be long enough."

She didn't even seem put out by his ill humor. His eyebrows rose slightly as he stared at her.

"Daddy?" Justin asked, jerking on his jeans.

"What, son?"

"What are we gonna eat for dinner? We're hungry."

Leslie looked down at the identical pairs of brown eyes. The boys were cute, but something in the looks they were giving her made her wonder about their guilelessness.

After an awkward silence, she said, "I could fix you something if your father doesn't mind." She allowed her gaze to only glance off the man still standing by the sink. He was even sexier than his voice had promised.

"That's not necessary—"

The children drowned him out with their excited questions.

"Can you make cookies?" one of the twins demanded, a smile on his face, as if he already knew the answer.

"I told you I could," she said, raising one brow.

"That was you?" the boys asked, excited looks on their faces.

"What do you mean?" the man growled. "What is she talking about, Gareth?"

"Didn't you tell your father about my phone call?" Leslie asked, looking from one twin to the other. Their brown eyes widened to give them a look of innocence, but Leslie wasn't fooled. She turned to their father. "I'm sorry, Mr. Graybow. I thought you were expecting me."

"What are you talking about? What phone call? Boys, what have you done this time?"

"But, Daddy, she can make cookies."

"And she said she likes little boys," Justin added.

The frustration and anger in the man's brown eyes, quite like his sons', gave Leslie the answer to whatever question she might ask. The man wasn't interested in hiring her, even on a temporary basis.

"Sorry, guys. I guess this was a bad idea." She smiled at the little boys and turned to go.

"But what are we going to eat for dinner? Daddy gots his hand in the sink, and we're hungry," one of the twins repeated.

Leslie hesitated. Though she recognized their plea as one of manipulation, she wouldn't mind a little dinner herself. It was a long drive back to town. "I make a very good grilled-cheese sandwich. If your father doesn't mind, I could fix some."

Though seemingly reluctant, the man at the sink gave an abrupt nod and the boys cheered.

For the next few minutes, they were her guides around the large kitchen. Leslie didn't find it as well stocked as she would have expected, but she opened a can of soup and heated it on the stove as she made the sandwiches.

The entire time she worked—efficiently, she hoped—the head of the household stood by the sink, his hand under the cold water, glaring at her.

What was his problem? Was he afraid she intended to charge him for her efforts? Maybe they couldn't afford a housekeeper now. She didn't know much about ranching, but she supposed a rancher, just like any other businessman, could have sudden catastrophes that affected his cash flow. That would explain the reason for the lack of supplies, too.

That thought sent her sharp glance to him. She noticed his shirt was missing a button, his hair was a little shaggy and his boots well-worn.

Leslie's irritation melted at once. How terrible not to be able to provide adequately for his family. Since money wasn't one of the difficulties she faced, she could afford to be generous. But tactful. She'd be very tact-ful.

After the boys had each received their dinner, she fixed two more sandwiches, one for her and one for the angry man staring at her.

"It's been about half an hour, Mr. Graybow. I think you can safely take your hand out of the water."

"The damn thing's frozen," he muttered.

Leslie was waiting with a towel and reached out to wrap the chilled skin in it. With a growl, Doug snatched it from her.

"I can do it."

The sympathetic tolerance she'd been silently ex-tending to him the past half hour almost completely disappeared. She stepped back and gestured to the ta-ble.

"Your dinner is ready. I hope you don't object to my eating also. I didn't eat supper before I came out here." But she took nothing for granted, standing stiff and proper until he offered her a seat.

Doug almost groaned aloud. He knew he'd been a bear. Standing there in pain, watching her prance around his kitchen, charming the hell out of his kids, when he'd already told her to get lost, was almost more than he could stand. Now, after fixing a meal, she ex-pected him to kick her out? He must've been worse than he'd thought.

"Of course I don't mind," he muttered and warily circled her and the table until it was between them.

As they both sat down, the boys, having already begun eating and taken the edge off their hunger, looked up.

"What's your name?" Gareth asked, his mouth full of sandwich.

"Leslie Hibbets," she replied as she laid the napkin in her lap.

Doug, having reached for his sandwich, instead picked up his napkin. "Boys, put your napkins in your laps."

He wasn't going to have Miss Prim and Proper thinking they had no manners.

"But, Daddy, we don't—" Gareth began.

"And, Gareth, don't talk with your mouth full," he hurriedly added. Both boys muttered apologies and he stared at the woman in triumph. She ignored him and smiled warmly at his children.

"Leslie," Justin said, staring at her in return.

"Yes?"

"I just wanted to say your name. It's pretty, like you."

"Why, thank you. What's your name?"

"I'm Justin and that's Gareth. But mostly people can't tell us apart."

Gareth giggled. "Our Sunday school teacher hates that. She makes us wear name tags." He giggled again. "But sometimes we switch and she doesn't know."

"Some people just call us 'the twins' 'cause they don't know which is which," Justin supplied.

"Yeah, and some people call us 'the twins from hell,'" Gareth added with another giggle.

She flashed a look, one eyebrow lifted, at their father. He glared back at her.

Hell, what was he supposed to do about the trouble the twins got into while he was trying to run a ranch? He never abandoned them. But cowboys who could handle the toughest bull seemed to disintegrate when left with these two.

"Gareth, eat your dinner," he snapped and stared at the woman, silently daring her to complain.

Though she met his look with all the coldness of a Wyoming blizzard, she said nothing.

With a sigh, he picked up the sandwich. He didn't much feel like defending his parental performance. Not when it had been seven hours since lunch. And those hours had been spent on horseback, rounding up the herd to draw them closer to the barns.

Before he even realized it, the soft golden cheese and toasted bread had melted into his mouth. He finished off the soup just as quickly, still hungry. The boys, too, had had a busy day and they had also cleaned their plates.

"Why don't I make some more sandwiches?" Miss Hibbets offered the boys with a smile. Their eager nods reflected his own thoughts. He only hoped she intended to include him as a recipient of those additional sandwiches.

He had his answer almost at once. She rose from the table, but before moving away she held out her plate to him. "I haven't touched the other half of my sandwich. Would you like to eat it while I fix more? There's no need for it to get cold."

"Thanks," he replied, reaching for the food. He wasn't one to cut off his nose to spite his face.

With such generosity on her part, Doug let go of some of his animosity. The woman was a lot better than he'd expected. Besides being attractive, she knew her way around the kitchen and seemed to like his children. She would've been a perfect housekeeper. Too bad she didn't answer *that* ad. He would've hired her in a minute.

When he realized his gaze was fastened on how rounded and smooth her hips filled out the jeans she was wearing, he changed his mind. Nope, he couldn't even hire her as a housekeeper. He might not be able to keep his hands out of the cookie jar. And then he'd find himself facing marriage again.

She turned toward the table, carrying a plate of sandwiches, and his gaze moved up her body, watching the thrust of her breasts through the blue sweater she wore. He'd been without a woman too long, he assured himself hastily as he looked back down at his empty plate.

It was a good thing this woman would be leaving in a few minutes.

After they'd eaten their fill, with Doug keeping his gaze trained on his plate, Leslie insisted on cleaning the kitchen. Since that was one of Doug's least favorite chores, he agreed to her offer and chased the twins upstairs for their baths.

"Leslie, don't leave without coming to tell us bye, please?" Justin pleaded as he climbed the steps.

"Yeah! You can read us a story. Daddy's always too tired," Gareth chimed in.

"Only if it's a short story. I have a long drive back to the motel," she promised with that warm smile she reserved for his sons.

Not that he cared. He wasn't looking for that kind of tenderness.

Fifteen minutes later, she joined them in the boys' bedroom, read one of their stories and then told the boys good-night, adding how much she'd enjoyed meeting them.

Doug was irritated when Justin's eyes watered and he asked the woman if she couldn't stay. He felt guilty, as if he didn't love his sons enough to provide them with a mother. But, damn it, he just couldn't!

He hurried down the stairs, anxious to rid the place of the curvaceous brunette who lured his sons with her smile and tempted him with her body.

"Mr. Graybow?" she said in a low voice, just behind him. "Before I leave, could we talk?"

Standing at the bottom of the stairs, he turned to watch her reach his side. "If it's about a phone call, I gather the boys led you to think you should come here. I'm sorry if it was an inconvenience, but, believe me, there's nothing to talk about."

"I think there is," she replied, tilting her chin up at him.

If they'd been lovers, it would've been a challenge he wouldn't refuse. His lips would cover hers and he'd wrap his arms around—

"Look, Miss Hibbets, I told you the ad was a mistake."

"I know. But I think I've figured out why you placed the ad and now say it's a mistake. And I believe I have a solution to the difficulty."

Doug stared at the woman as if she had two heads. She knew about the responses he'd had to that ridiculous ad? About his aversion to those desperate women? To any woman who intended to lock him into marriage just for security?

"It's nothing to be embarrassed about," she said in a soothing manner, as if she were calming him.

"You know about the pictures?" he finally had to ask in a strangled voice.

"What pictures?" she asked, tilting her head to one side and frowning in puzzlement.

"The—the other applicants sent pictures."

"You want a picture from me?"

"No!" he gasped even as his mind flashed some possibilities.

He turned his back to her, unable to face her if she thought those pictures of women in incredibly suggestive, revealing poses weren't something to be embarrassed about. Or intended to offer some of her own.

"Mr. Graybow," she began again when he remained silent, "I like your little boys and this is what I really want. I promise I won't be too demanding about—"

"Leave my children out of this discussion! I won't have them a part of it. In fact, I don't want to talk about any of this." He chanced one look at her creamy complexion, her full lips, trembling with some undefined emotion. How could she look like such an angel and approve of those pictures?

"I'm trying to explain to you—"

He whirled back around. "What does it take to get through to you, lady? We don't want you here."

"But you haven't even asked about my qualifications," she protested, her cheeks flushed.

Her fingers moved to the first button on her sweater and Doug panicked. She hadn't sent pictures. She meant to reveal herself right here, right now! He grabbed her raised hand and captured the other one that had remained by her side. "Don't even think about it!" His voice was husky, a mixture of horror and undeniable interest.

Now almost nose to nose, he watched as shock filled her eyes.

"Turn loose of me!" She twisted in his hold, foolishly trying to escape his strong grip.

His fingers burned as they touched her soft skin, and he jerked away from her before he gave in to temptation. "Gladly. All I want you to do is go."

She backed away from him, her blue eyes still wide. "You've convinced me, Mr. Graybow. Just—just let me get my jacket and purse and I'll leave."

He frowned as he realized he'd actually scared her. "I didn't mean to hurt you."

She didn't answer but kept her gaze pinned on him, as if she expected him to attack at any moment. Picking up her coat and purse, she edged toward the door.

Doug felt like a first-class heel. He would never hurt a woman. But he couldn't stand there and let her strip. Moving toward the door to open it for her, he came to an abrupt halt when she stepped back.

"I'm just opening the door, I promise."

"I can do that," she assured him breathlessly, her gaze still glued to him.

"This is ridiculous, Miss Hibbets. I wasn't trying to hurt you."

"Fine. I'm leaving now, Mr. Graybow. But I'd appreciate it if you'd keep your distance." When he remained in place, she continued moving to the door.

With one hand behind her back, she turned the doorknob and started outside.

Over her shoulder, Doug stared at the illuminated circle made by the porch light and knew he couldn't let her leave. "Damn!"

LESLIE WAS ON THE VERGE of turning her back on the demented man and racing for her car when she heard his expletive. Shocked, she looked at his face and then turned away. She had no time to spare.

"Stop! You can't leave, Miss Hibbets. It's too dangerous!" he called.

She assumed he was referring to the snow falling thickly. It had started snowing shortly after she started for the ranch, but she'd forgotten about it because of all that had happened. Now, there was already almost half a foot on her car. But she would choose snow over the man behind her any day.

Though she slowed to maintain her footing, she never stopped. She'd be all right once she got into her car and locked the door.

She was down the steps, with her car parked only a few feet away, when one of those strong hands grabbed her arm, preventing her departure.

"Stop, Miss Hibbets. It isn't safe!"

Automatically she wrenched her arm from his hold. When, only seconds later, she touched the door handle, she knew she'd won.

As she did, she heard a large crash. Keeping her hand on the door, she looked over her shoulder to see Mr. Graybow lying in the snow at the bottom of the steps. He wasn't moving. Holding her breath, she leaned slightly toward him. "Are you okay?"

His only answer was a groan.

"Mr. Graybow, I'm not going to fall for any of your tricks. You might as well get up."

He muttered something and tried to stand up, then fell back again with an even louder moan.

"Mr. Graybow?" Was the man a total klutz? First he burned his hand and now he fell down the stairs. And what was she supposed to do about it?

"I can't— I might've broken something," the man gasped.

That she could believe. It hurt to even look at his lean, muscular leg bent at an odd angle.

"Is there anyone I can call for help?"

"B-bunkhouse," he muttered, his voice shaking, either from pain or the wet snow beginning to cover him.

Though she could dimly make out another building with a light burning, she decided the easiest way to summon help would be to use her car horn. Opening the door, she slid beneath the wheel, ignoring the temptation to drive away from this nightmare. Grateful for the Girl Scouts of her youth, she tapped out SOS.

Though it only took a couple of minutes for a response, they were the longest two minutes of her life. A distant door was slammed open and she finally heard the welcome sound of voices and footsteps.

"What the hell's goin' on?" one of the men shouted as he reached the area lit by the porch light.

Leslie was standing by her car door. She stepped forward. "Mr. Graybow fell. I think he's broken his leg."

"Ma'am," the man said, tipping his hat even as he went down on one knee by his employer.

"Boss? You break a leg?"

"I don't—damn," Graybow said and then gasped. "The thing hurts like hell."

"Curly, go get the four-wheeler," the man said to one of the cowboys. "It's about all that will get through tonight."

A man, supposedly Curly, ran away, and the other man turned his attention to Leslie. "Ma'am, would you

go get some blankets from the house? Maybe a sleepin'
bag, too, and a pillow.''

She started to explain that she wouldn't know where
to look, but the man bent back toward his boss, assuming she would follow his orders. With a shrug, she
stepped carefully over the injured man and climbed the
steps to open the front door.

Two pairs of brown eyes stared at her from the bottom of the stairs. ''Leslie!'' Justin cried, leaping up and
running to wrap his arms around her legs. ''You didn't
go.''

Gareth followed his brother and Leslie found it impossible to move. ''Boys, I need your help. Your father
fell, and I need to find some blankets to keep him
warm.''

Gareth ran off to find the items she'd mentioned, but
Justin stayed by her side.

''Is Daddy hurt bad?''

She knelt down beside him. ''The ranch hands have
come to help him. I'm sure he'll be all right as soon as
we get him warm.''

Justin took her hand and led her after Gareth. With
the boys' expert guidance, it only took a couple of
minutes to round up the items. The boys followed her
to the door, but she made them stay inside in spite of
their protests.

The Jeep pulled up just as she reached the bottom of
the stairs.

''Here. I found everything.''

The cowboy ignored her as he gestured for the other
men to help him lift Graybow.

''Shouldn't you splint the leg before you move him?''
she asked, concerned in spite of herself.

''Lady, we got to get him out of this blizzard!''

She covered her ears when Doug Graybow gave a mangled cry of pain as he was moved. Fortunately for him, he passed out before they got him into the vehicle.

His cry brought both boys tumbling down the steps, their footed pajamas immediately wet from the snow. "Daddy?" they cried, terror in their voices.

Leslie turned and scooped both of them into her arms and lifted them back to the porch. "Your dad is going to be fine. It just hurt when they moved him."

"Daddy don't never complain when he's hurt," Gareth assured her.

Leslie could believe that statement. He seemed like the kind of male who could never admit a weakness. Look at how he had refused to listen to her offer because he was embarrassed at not having money for a housekeeper.

"Excuse me, ma'am, but who are you?" the cowboy who seemed to be in charge asked.

"Leslie cooked us dinner," Justin assured him.

"I—" Leslie began, sure he would demand more of an explanation.

"Oh, a friend. Well, could you stay with the boys? It'll take two of us to get him to town, and the other two will have to carry on in the morning, so if you don't mind—" He turned as another moan came from the truck. "Okay?"

Without waiting for her agreement, he leapt down several steps and slid behind the wheel of the truck.

"Wait! I—"

But in seconds the Jeep had completely disappeared in the falling snow, abandoning her to care for two little boys she scarcely knew.

Chapter Three

"You'll stay with us, won't you, Leslie?" Justin's eyes as well as his voice pleaded with her. But it was the look on his face that decided her.

"Yes, of course I will," she said, "and the first thing we have to do is get the two of you out of those wet pajamas. Inside, at once."

Her mind was filled with all kinds of questions, but they were never asked. Instead, she put the boys in a steaming tub of water and went downstairs to make hot chocolate.

An hour later, she finally tucked the boys in their beds, sitting with them until they drifted off to sleep. Though they'd tried to show their bravery, she'd seen through their pretense and had wanted to reassure them. In spite of their mischief about the phone call, they were still little children.

Then she gathered the wet pajamas and found the laundry room downstairs. Rather than just wash those two items, she did a full load from the big pile of laundry that almost covered the entire floor.

And the man didn't need a housekeeper? Ha!

Next, she returned to the kitchen and tidied up the dirty dishes from their late snack. She put the last clean cup on the shelf and closed the cabinet.

Now what? A wave of exhaustion hit her and she realized it was almost eleven o'clock. Well, eleven o'clock Kansas City time. The time her body was used to. Obviously Mr. Graybow was not going to return tonight, so she might as well make herself comfortable.

The only other room with sheets on the bed was the master bedroom. She supposed she could locate some linen and make up one of the other beds, but she was too tired. After all, she'd driven all the way from Kansas early that morning. Not to mention she'd met the charming Mr. D. Graybow, cooked his dinner, argued and been left in charge of his twins.

She stared at the big bed. It would serve him right if she slept in his bed! Visions of Goldilocks danced through her mind. But Mr. Graybow wasn't going to get home until tomorrow sometime. So what harm could there be?

She was going to make herself comfortable and he could just lump it if he didn't like it. Filled with righteous indignation, she marched toward the big bed.

She even went so far as to wear one of his T-shirts to sleep. She'd have it washed and put back before he ever returned.

With a sigh, she slid into his big bed and pulled the covers up to her nose. *Well, Leslie Hibbets,* she said to herself, *you wanted to be connected to someone, to find some excitement.* She smiled. *Mission accomplished.*

"GOOD MORNING, Mr. Graybow," a cheery voice said, piercing the fog that surrounded him.

Doug slowly moved his head toward the sound, but he had difficulty lifting his eyelids.

"How are you feeling this morning?"

He struggled to hold on to his temper. Since he felt as though he'd been hit by a truck, he thought the sunshiny voice was highly inappropriate. "Terrible," he muttered.

"Can you open your eyes?"

"I don't think so."

"Please try. The doctor will be here soon."

What little patience he had suddenly disappeared. "You can tell the doctor—"

"Careful, Doug," a male voice interrupted. "You'll embarrass my nurse."

Some of his tension disappeared as Doug recognized an old friend's voice. "Jim, what happened?"

"Open your eyes and I'll tell you."

With monumental effort, Doug managed that task and then quickly shut them again as the bright lights brought pain surging through his head.

"The lights," he protested faintly.

"Madge, turn off the overhead lights until his eyes adjust a little."

Doug heard the click of a light switch and he tried again. This time he gradually got his eyes open and focused on Jim Kelsey, the doctor in Riverside. "What happened?"

"I'm not real clear. Moss and Curly brought you in a little before midnight, said you fell down your front steps and broke your leg. There's also the matter of a slight concussion."

"Damn. I remember now. That blasted woman!"

"Woman? Is your social life picking up?"

"Yeah, thanks to Ben and Will."

"What do they have to do with it?"

"They put an ad in the paper to get me a wife. I've been advertising for a housekeeper for a month with no response. They thought they'd improve on my offer."

The doctor laughed. "Get any responses?"

Doug could feel his face reddening. "Some you wouldn't believe. Then, last night, this woman turns up on my doorstep. Came all the way from Kansas, expecting me to marry her, I guess." A sudden thought made him frown and increased the pain in his head. "Did she come into town with me last night?"

"I only saw Moss and Curly. They slept here at the hospital 'cause of the storm."

"Damn! I bet she's still at the ranch with the boys. Where's Moss?" he demanded, rising as if to get out of the bed.

"Hold it, Doug. You're not going anywhere. I'll find Moss and Curly for you, but you need to stay here until tomorrow."

"Jim, if that woman is out there with my kids, I'm going back this morning, if I have to crawl to get there. You don't understand what these women are like. They're desperate!"

The doctor frowned and reached for Doug's wrist to take his pulse. Then he pushed the button to summon the nurse. "Madge," he ordered when she appeared, "go find Curly and Moss and have them come here."

Again Doug struggled to get up.

"Doug, you can't get out of bed. We haven't set your leg because of the swelling."

Doug gave his physician a pained smile. "Well, Doc, I reckon I'd better find a way of getting around because there are some things that just can't wait."

The doctor smiled, as if enjoying himself. "That's why Madge left that bedpan handy. If you hurry, you can take care of business before company arrives."

Doug glared at him.

"Boss, I STILL THINK this is crazy. The lady seemed nice last night. I'm sure the boys are fine." Moss was following in the tracks of the snowplow down the snowy road to the ranch.

"One of the boys said she cooked dinner last night," Curly added helpfully.

"Just hurry," Doug ordered through gritted teeth. He didn't feel like making conversation. His leg was in a temporary brace and he'd had to be carried to the truck. Jim had thrown in a pair of crutches at the last minute but had warned him to use them only for trips to the bathroom. At least he hadn't offered a bedpan again.

In four or five days, Doug would have to return so they could put his leg in a cast. Until then he had to stay in bed. Great! Now, one of his cowboys would have to play nursemaid, and they'd be two men shorter than they already were.

It was all that woman's fault. Things had been going along just fine until she arrived. Honesty forced him to rephrase that statement. They'd been surviving until she arrived. They could've used a housekeeper, of course, but he'd just about given up on that plan.

"Who *was* that lady? The one you're so worried about," Moss asked, checking in the rearview mirror for his boss's response.

"Uh, she's a visitor."

"Mighty pretty," Curly said, turning to grin over his shoulder.

"She's okay," Doug muttered. He didn't want to discuss her, or think about her, or remember her warmth, her curves, her cooking.

"Hey! Maybe she came in response to that ad!" Moss suddenly exclaimed, a big grin on his weathered face. "You know, the one Ben and Will—" His glance met Doug's in the rearview mirror and he suddenly stopped talking. He'd known Doug long enough to recognize the danger signals.

Curly, too, looked at Doug and said nothing.

Moss cleared his throat. "Uh, want us to move the herd closer in, since the snow's let up? It'd make it easier to feed them."

Doug concurred with his suggestion, and any other conversation for the rest of the ride dealt with work. The drive seemed interminable to Doug, every jolt shooting pain through his entire body. Jim had given him pain pills, but he refused to take any until he made sure he had that woman out of his home.

He'd need his wits about him to get rid of her. Especially if she'd spent the past few hours charming his boys as she had done last night.

He'd checked himself out of the hospital long before he should've, according to Jim, who protested his decision, but Doug wasn't going to let a little red tape interfere with protecting his children. When they reached the ranch house, Moss pulled the Jeep as close to the steps as possible behind the woman's car. She was still here.

The two ranch hands both came to his door, opened it and began to ease him forward on the seat. He gritted his teeth at the pain.

"Easy, boss, we got you," Moss muttered.

They carried him up the steps, his broken leg stuck straight out in front of him. Curly managed to get the front door open and they backed into the warmth of the hall. Silence greeted them.

"Where is everyone?" Curly asked, but Doug had just about reached the end of his patience. His leg was aching big-time.

"Just take me up to bed. Then we'll sort everything out."

They made their way up the stairs and Moss shoved open the door to his room. The two cowboys stopped in their tracks, and Doug, clinging to their broad shoulders, looked up to see what the holdup was.

What he saw was a rather shapely female posterior. Leslie Hibbets snapped to attention and whirled around. Before she could sputter anything, the boys came racing around the bed.

"Daddy!" Leslie stepped in their path before they could crash into the cowboys holding their father.

"You can see your dad in a minute. I think we'd better finish his bed first so he can lie down. You've been such super helpers, your dad will be so proud."

Instead of the frightened faces he expected, his sons beamed at him and then scurried back to the other side of the bed. They never obeyed him like that! Stunned, he watched the lady also turn away. That was when he realized she'd been bent over his bed, making it up.

"What are you doing?" he demanded, all the frustration he felt evident in his voice.

She turned around again and stared at him. All warmth was gone from her blue eyes. "I used your bed last night. So I washed the sheets this morning and now we're putting them back on." There was a challenge in there, as if daring him to complain.

"Wow! You must've been up early," Moss said before Doug could speak. His voice fairly dripped with admiration, but Doug suspected it had nothing to do with her early rise. She looked just as sexy this morning in her tight jeans as she had last night.

Her smile didn't lessen her sexiness.

"Not too early. The boys said they always get up at six." As if just now remembering the two cowboys were still holding him, she hurried back to her bedmaking.

"You lucky devil," Moss muttered in Doug's ear. Doug glared at him.

"Each of you get a pillow," Leslie ordered his children, and they hurried to follow her orders.

What had she done—hypnotized them?

"Now you can put Mr. Graybow in bed," she suggested to Moss and Curly, stepping back out of the way.

As eager as his body was to make the acquaintance of something soft and stationary, Doug wasn't a happy camper. For some reason, he grew less so as the fresh smell of clean sheets hit him. He hadn't bothered with such niceties since Agnes left. He hadn't had time, he defended himself, as he closed his eyes and relaxed for just a moment.

"Does he have any medicine he's supposed to take?" that lilting voice asked, and his eyes popped open.

"Yeah, some pain pills," Moss answered before he could stop him.

"I don't need them."

All three adults gave him a derisive look.

"Do you hurt, Daddy?" Gareth asked, leaning toward him.

He'd never lied to his children. Well, almost never. Only for their own good. "A little, son."

"Then you should take your medicine or you won't get better. 'Member? You told us."

Leslie walked into his bathroom and he heard the water run.

"I'm going to be fine," he told his son, trying to inject a heartiness into his voice to convince him. The headache pounding at his temples made it difficult, though.

"Here's some water, sweetie. Maybe if you help your dad, he'll take his medicine. I'm sure he's not afraid since he's so big and strong."

Even though there wasn't a hint of laughter in her voice, the snickers from his men told him he was right on target when he thought she was making fun of him.

"Here's the medicine, Justin. You hand it to him and then Gareth can give him the water," Moss said helpfully.

Doug had no choice but to follow orders.

"Have you two already had breakfast? We were going to have pancakes and you're welcome to join us," Leslie offered the cowboys, that warm smile on her lips.

His gut clinched as he watched his men explain that they'd been dragged away from the hospital before eating. Without even a glance in his direction, Leslie led the drooling men from his room.

"Do you want some pancakes, Daddy? We'll bring you some," Justin said, patting his father's cheek.

At least *someone* hadn't forgotten him. Not that he wanted Leslie Hibbets to think about him. Of course not. But Moss and Curly could at least remember he was alive.

"No, son, but thanks for offering. I believe I'll just sleep. You two will be all right, won't you? You won't get into trouble?"

"'Course not, Daddy," Gareth said. "Leslie's here."

His mind was growing cloudy and his lips didn't seem to work too well, but there was something he needed to say. Something about Leslie. Laughter floated up the stairs as he slid into unconsciousness. Yes. There was definitely something about Leslie.

LESLIE POURED MOSS a second cup of coffee and returned to her chair. They'd enjoyed a big breakfast. In between bites, the two men had filled Leslie in on the doctor's diagnosis.

"So Mr. Graybow is going to have to remain in bed for four or five days? Who will take care of him?" she asked.

"I guess we'll have to take turns, though we were already short a hand before the boss got hurt. That will make us twice as short."

Moss glared at his friend, Leslie noticed, when Curly started to speak.

"Maybe you can hire someone to take care of him." She thought again about the man upstairs refusing to hire her because he was short of money. The hospital bills wouldn't help.

"Well, it's kind of difficult..." Moss began and then trailed off, looking as if he wasn't sure how much he should reveal.

"Look, I'd volunteer," she began, but before Moss's grin could spread too wide, she added, "but it wouldn't work."

"What do you mean?" Curly asked. "It'd be perfect."

"No, it wouldn't. Mr. Graybow doesn't want me here."

"He hasn't tasted your pancakes," Moss said, his smile still in place.

She chuckled but shook her head no. "Thanks for the compliment, but he made his wishes clear last night."

"Last night, he thought he could manage. It's pretty obvious now that he can't." Moss watched her reaction.

"We can't cook for Daddy, Leslie. How will he get something to eat if you don't stay?" Gareth asked.

"And us, too. You promised to bake cookies," Justin reminded her.

Leslie knew the boys were trying to manipulate her into feeling sorry for them. They'd already suggested several times that she should stay.

Not that she disagreed with them. She hadn't been sure what she'd been looking for when she set out on her travels, but a home and family were definitely on the list. This job would be perfect for a few months. She could try out being a mom, see if she really wanted children. The cowboys seemed nice, too. She might even meet that special man she had dreamed of. There certainly seemed to be enough men around to choose from. Immediate thoughts of the one upstairs were hurriedly dismissed.

"I thought we'd have time..." she began in response to the child's reminder.

Justin's mouth sagged and Leslie hesitated. "Maybe...maybe I could just stay until tomorrow. That would give you time to find someone, wouldn't it?" she asked Moss.

"And we could make cookies?" Justin asked.

She nodded to the child, bringing a smile back to his face.

"I'll sure try to find someone," Moss promised, his look as eager as the other three males in the room.

"I can do some extra cooking, too, to help out. Things that can be frozen," she added, her mind racing with the possibilities. "You do have someone to cook for you, don't you?" she asked Moss.

"Blackie cooks. But lately he's been having to be in the saddle most of the time. What with the shortage, you know. We're all mostly living off sandwiches."

"Sandwiches? After working outside in the cold all day?" she asked, horrified. She'd been cooking for her invalid mother, but she understood the appetites hard-working men could have. "I'll try to help out while I'm here."

"That'd be great," Moss said as he stood.

"But there's not a lot of supplies here," she hurriedly added, knowing once the two men left the kitchen she wouldn't be able to ask any more questions. They'd be out in the cold, working.

"Blackie just got a full order in three days ago. I bet the boss didn't get around to taking his share of it. You go on down to the bunkhouse and get whatever you need. The boys will show you."

"All right. I'll try to have something fixed for dinner when you get in."

They grinned at her and stepped out onto the snowy porch. As they walked down the steps, Curly said to his friend, "Man, how did we get so lucky?"

Leslie shook her head. The grouch upstairs wasn't going to think her staying was luck. Unless it was the bad kind. But what could she do? He certainly couldn't take care of anything since he had to stay in bed. And she was just staying until they found someone else.

"Yeah, right," she muttered to herself as she retraced her steps to the kitchen. Somehow she didn't think Moss thought it would be that easy, in spite of the smile he'd given her. If it were, why hadn't Doug Graybow already filled the position he'd advertised for?

She told the boys to clear the table while she checked on their father. With a few grumbles, they started carrying the dishes to the dishwasher. After several minutes of working in silence, Justin whispered, "Do you think she'll stay?"

"Maybe. But how come we have to work? I thought a mommy was supposed to take care of us," Gareth complained.

"I know, but... but I kind of like her. I think she'd make a good mommy. She smells better'n Agnes."

"Yeah, but she hasn't made any cookies yet. If she doesn't make cookies, she can't be *my* mommy," Gareth declared, his jaw squared in determination just like his father's.

"Okay. She has to make cookies," Justin agreed. "But do you think Daddy will let her stay?"

"I don't know. Maybe we just won't tell him."

"I think he'll find out. He always does. And then we get in trouble. How about we let him have some of the cookies? I bet he likes 'em, too."

"Okay, but not too many. I'm *this* hungry for cookies," Gareth exclaimed, flinging his arms wide. Unfortunately, he forgot about the glass in his hand, and it went flying across the kitchen to shatter against the cabinet.

"Uh-oh."

LESLIE EASED OPEN the bedroom door and looked in. Doug Graybow lay sprawled out on the big bed, his eyes closed.

"Mr. Graybow?" she whispered.

When there was no response, she crept over to the bed. He was a big man, his hard, muscled body covering much of the mattress. Even in sleep he looked powerful.

A shiver ran over her, and she took an involuntary step backward. As if recognizing her presence, he stirred and groaned. Afraid she'd wakened him, she froze, not relaxing until his breathing evened out again. Then she frowned.

The doctor had obviously split the seam on his jeans since the material flapped around the temporary brace. But he couldn't be comfortable with those tight jeans around his waist. She should have had him remove them before taking his medicine.

She looked around the room, as if seeking help. If he were a woman, she wouldn't hesitate to make him more comfortable. Maybe she could get the twins... No, they weren't strong enough.

The cowboys wouldn't be back until dark.

That left only her.

If only she could just think of the man as her patient, not as a hunk of masculinity that would make many a female heart swoon. She remembered the way he'd looked when he'd first opened the door to her. Even then, with that ferocious frown, she'd registered his sex appeal.

"Stop that!" she whispered to herself. When he didn't stir, she stepped closer to the bed. Leaning over him, she inched his T-shirt up from his waist, her fingers brushing against warm flesh.

Just below his belly button, centered on a flat, hard stomach, were the buttons to his jeans. She licked her dry lips and then reached to unfasten them. The jeans were tight and she had to struggle to push each button through its hole. A sigh of relief escaped when she felt his cotton briefs beneath her fingers. She wasn't sure what she would've done had he been one of those men who didn't bother with underwear.

Standing up, Leslie stretched her neck, stiff with the tension of the past few minutes. Now all she had to do was slide the jeans down those long, lean legs. She tried to ignore the butterflies in her stomach.

As if in relief that the tight jeans were loosened, Doug shifted on the bed. Leslie jumped as if he'd opened his eyes. "Oh!"

She waited until he settled again before moving to the end of the bed. With the covers pulled back, she thought she could pull the pant legs and the jeans would slip off.

A minute later she realized her theory wasn't working. After studying the situation, she eased onto the bed. With a cautious look at his smooth, relaxed features, she straddled him and lifted his hips, pulling the jeans at the same time.

Just as she was congratulating herself on the success of the operation, large hands spanned her waist and pulled her forward. With her heart thumping like mad, unable to breathe, she found herself wrapped in Doug Graybow's arms, pressed against his lean length.

He muttered something in her ear, but she couldn't distinguish his words over her own heart beating. As she was about to protest loudly and shove against her captor's hold, she realized his eyes were closed.

Could he still be asleep?

She waited on tenterhooks for him to move again. When he didn't, she eased back from his embrace. With a sigh of relief, she decided he had no idea what had happened. Apparently, her rather intimate position over him had awakened some memory.

Her cheeks burned but at least the man wouldn't remember.

She slipped off the bed and returned to the foot of it. Now that the jeans were below his hips, she was able to pull them off without any difficulty. She tried to keep her eyes firmly fastened to the denim material, but the stark white briefs and the warm skin drew her gaze.

She might have lingered if it hadn't been for the shattering of glass in the kitchen below.

Hurriedly, she whisked the cover over his now-bare legs and ran from the room.

Chapter Four

After a trip to the bunkhouse where Leslie started a pot of stew for the cowboys' dinner and gathered supplies to bring back, she and the twins returned to the house.

"Are we going to make the cookies now, Leslie?" Justin asked anxiously as they entered the house.

"In just a minute. We should check on your dad first." Before she could say anything else, the boys set down their sacks and ran for the stairs. "Quietly," she called. "He may still be sleeping."

She checked her watch as she followed the boys. Probably he wouldn't stir for another couple of hours. At least she hoped so. That would give her time to fix lunch and make cookies with the boys—and recover from the embarrassment of undressing their father.

When she reached the bedroom door, the boys were standing by the bed, whispering. Doug Graybow didn't even flicker an eyelash at the noise. He was obviously still in a deep sleep. Probably the best thing for him since Moss had told her he had a mild concussion.

"Okay, boys. Go hang up your coats and wash your hands and we'll make cookies," she whispered. Like twin tornadoes, the two moved past her and out of sight.

She stood there in the relative quiet, staring at the unconscious man. The urge to smooth his brow, to adjust his covers, grew stronger the longer she watched. With an abrupt nod to no one in particular, she pulled the door to, then drew a deep breath.

She was only going to be here a day or two. Moss would find someone. Of course he would. And then she'd be on her way back to Kansas to get on with her life—whatever that might be.

In spite of everything, Mr. D. Graybow had made it clear he didn't want her working for him. So she wouldn't. She'd find a place for herself, somewhere she'd be happy. It just wouldn't be here.

And that was just as well. The man was as sexy as sin, even with a concussion and a broken leg. Another deep breath helped her clear her head of such ridiculous thoughts. Which was a good thing, because the boys' room door opened and the two whirlwinds were beaming up at her, extending their hands for approval.

DOUG SLOWLY BECAME conscious of his surroundings. His room. Not the hospital. Why had he thought— The pain that shot up his leg when he tried to move it answered that question.

Along with that bit of information came the rest of it. The woman, his chasing her, then his fall. The hospital with Jim Kelsey fussing over him. Then his arrival back home to find the woman making his bed with clean sheets, charming his boys into instant obedience and shaming him into taking his medicine.

At least she was long gone. Moss knew what he wanted, and he could rely on Moss to carry out his orders. He looked at the window and figured he had an hour or two before his workers would return to the bunkhouse. Probably the boys were down there with Blackie.

He looked around him for the crutches Jim had given him. As much as he'd hated that damn bedpan, he kind of wished he had it here now. Getting to the crutches leaning against the wall by the door wasn't going to be easy.

But he didn't have much choice. He sure couldn't wait a couple of hours.

Throwing back the covers, he slid to the side of the bed. Since he couldn't bend his leg because of the brace, he was debating whether he should slide on the floor to the crutches, or hop on his good leg, when the door opened.

"You're awake!" *that woman* exclaimed.

Red suffused his cheeks as he grabbed the covers. He suddenly realized he was only wearing his briefs and a T-shirt.

"Yes, I'm awake. Where are my jeans?" He could've sworn he'd had them on when he got home. Looking at his visitor, he surprised a bright blush on her cheeks.

"I—I removed them. You couldn't get comfortable, they were so tight."

Now he was as embarrassed as she looked. Particularly as a lingering scent of her perfume filled his nostrils. He felt a vague stirring of some memory but it eluded him. Upset with both himself and her, he said suddenly, "What are you still doing here?"

He hadn't meant his question to sound so abrupt, so angry, but it had. He knew it by the way she stiffened.

"Taking care of you and your children until Moss can find someone else."

Doug grimaced. Moss knew there wasn't a snowball's chance in hell of finding someone to come take care of them. So what was he pulling?

"You agreed to do that?"

"Yes. I don't have to return home at once, and it seemed cruel to abandon the three of you."

"Yeah. Especially since it's your fault," he growled.

Her shoulders went rigid, drawing his attention to her full breasts. His mouth was suddenly dry.

"I don't quite see how your broken leg could be my fault."

"I've lived here thirty-two years, all my life, and never fallen down those stairs. I wouldn't have this time except you jerked away from me."

"Oh? So I should have let you paw me to keep you from breaking your leg?" She stood with her hands on her shapely hips, righteous anger on her face.

He stared back at her, trying to keep his gaze above her neck. "Paw you? I was trying to stop you from getting lost in a snowstorm!"

"It wasn't that bad and you know it! That's just an excuse!"

He gaped, unable to believe what she was saying. Finally he pushed himself as erect as he could manage. "Listen, lady, if I wanted to 'paw' someone, as you put it, there are plenty of women who would volunteer. I wouldn't have to settle for a—" He couldn't think how to finish his insult.

"Then call one of those numerous women to take care of you now. Because I'm not going to!" With a slam of the door, she disappeared from view, leaving him tense and upset. And stranded a long way from the bathroom.

"Wait!" he called and listened anxiously for returning footsteps. Nothing. Damn. His temper had gotten him in trouble again.

He leaned back against the pillow, drained by their argument, his headache returning.

"Hi, Daddy," the twins chorused as they opened the door.

"Boys." He sighed in relief. "Thanks for coming. Could you hand me my crutches?"

His children looked at each other. Then they shook their heads and started toward the bed, Gareth carefully carrying a glass.

"Boys! The crutches. You forgot the crutches. They're by the door," he said, his situation getting more desperate by the moment.

"Leslie said for you to take your medicine. She didn't say anything about you getting out of bed." Justin held out his hand, showing his father the pills he was carrying.

"Leslie is not the boss around here! I am!" he shouted before clutching his head. The stubborn looks on his children's faces told him he'd made a mistake. With a sigh, he quickly informed them why he needed his crutches and Justin laid down the pills on the bedside table and brought the crutches to his bed.

"Why didn't you ask Leslie?" he asked as he held them for his father.

"It was kind of embarrassing," Doug muttered, not bothering to explain that he'd insulted her before he thought to do so. And then it was too late.

After the difficult excursion to the bathroom, Doug was glad to settle back against the pillows. "Thanks, guys. How's everything going?"

After listening to their complaints the entire month since Agnes had departed, Doug expected more of the same. Instead, his children happily recounted their activities, with Leslie's name playing a large role in the recital.

"And we made the bestest cookies, Daddy," Justin assured him, a heavenly smile on his little face, as if he were munching on his favorite treat right then.

"And you didn't bring me one?" Doug teased, unable to resist the happiness his sons were showing.

"I'll go get you one," Justin promised fervently and rushed to the door.

"Bring him one I made, too," Gareth called, and then patted him on the shoulder. "Leslie showed us how to do it."

"That was nice of Leslie," he assured his son. The woman seemed to be a master at enslaving his children. Didn't she have them complaining about being bored? Getting into mischief? Begging her to read them a story?

Or maybe she had mesmerized them with the heavenly scents coming up the stairway. The house smelled better than it had when his mom was downstairs cooking.

"And you know what, Daddy?"

"No, Gareth. What?"

"Leslie can tell us apart. She don't never have to ask."

Doug could always tell them apart, but he and Moss were about the only ones. Somehow it seemed intrusive for Leslie to be able to. "How does she do that?"

"She said 'cause we're not the same person. And 'cause I have a freckle right here," Gareth said, pointing to his nose and chuckling.

Doug admired her perception, but he wasn't about to say so. His boys already seemed to adore the blasted woman.

Justin appeared in the doorway, but he wasn't alone. Standing behind him was Leslie, a tray in her hand. Her lips were tightened in a firm line and her gaze didn't meet his. "Justin wanted you to have a cookie, but I think you should eat something solid before you do."

He suddenly realized his stomach was empty. His last meal had been the sandwiches and soup she'd prepared last night. On his best behavior, he said, "Thank you. I'd appreciate that."

"If you'll sit up, the boys will fix the pillows behind your back," she instructed, still keeping her gaze on the tray.

Once more, he watched as his boys rushed to fulfill her every command. He frowned but tried to hide his irritation. After all, she was being nice to him. He leaned back against the pillows and thanked his children.

"Leslie says we're her best helpers," Justin announced proudly, leaning against his father's shoulder. "She doesn't know where anything is."

"Anything what?" Doug asked sharply, a sudden vision filling him of Leslie going through his belongings, trying to assess his net worth.

"All your hidden valuables, of course," the woman said coldly as she plopped the tray into his lap.

He flinched and grabbed the wobbling tray. Obviously she had understood his meaning even if his children hadn't.

"Boys, why don't you stay and keep your dad company while he eats, and I'll go down and put the vegetables in the stew."

"I thought you were leaving?" Doug couldn't help asking.

She halted on her way out of the room, but she kept her back to him. "I am. Just as soon as the cowboys get back. It would be irresponsible to leave the children alone."

"You're leaving?" Justin asked anxiously, taking a step toward her.

"Yes, sweetie. Remember, I told you earlier I couldn't stay. Now, take care of your daddy until I get back."

Both boys turned to glare at their father as soon as the door closed behind her.

"Daddy, we don't want her to leave! She makes great cookies!" Gareth complained.

Doug, on the other hand, wanted that woman gone, not mixing in his business, or worming her way into the hearts of his employees, like she had his children.

Yeah, he was glad to get rid of her. "Don't worry, boys, I'll find someone else to take care of us. We don't need Leslie. Bring me the phone."

"WHAT ARE WE GOING TO DO? She'll make a perfect mommy," Justin whispered. The twins were sitting on the stairs, waiting for Leslie's return.

"I don't know. Daddy doesn't like her. Don't daddies have to like the mommy?"

"Mrs. Meggy's husband likes her. He's always hugging on her. I saw him kiss her once."

"Daddy and Leslie was fightin'. She don't want to stay." Gareth rested his drooping chin in his hand. "And she didn't even fuss when I broke that glass."

"Yeah. Agnes would'a spanked you."

Both boys sighed in unison.

"There must be something we can do," Justin finally said.

"I don't know what," Gareth admitted and sighed again.

"Me neither...unless—" Justin broke off and stared at his brother.

"What?"

"We shouldn't."

"Shouldn't what?"

"Break her car. Then she couldn't leave."

"Hey, yeah! But how do we do it?"

"MRS. WILLIAMS? This is Doug Graybow at the Bar-G. I had an accident last night and—no, it's nothing serious, just a broken leg. Yes, thank you. The reason I'm calling is I need someone to take care of me and the twins for a— Mrs. Williams, I promise— Mrs. Williams?"

He hung up the receiver. Mrs. Williams made her feelings clear. And who could blame her after the fiasco the last time that she baby-sat? The twins had almost flooded the house.

Who else could he call? He'd talked to Ben, but he said Meggy wasn't feeling well.

The widow Hicks had gone to stay with her daughter in Chicago.

Mrs. White had told him she'd sprained her wrist, but Doug didn't believe her. She prided herself on keeping everything in its place, and his twins wouldn't cooperate.

He'd even called the pastor of his church, but the man had had no idea of anyone who could help. When Doug had admitted that Leslie had stayed overnight to help, the pastor had suggested he plead with her to stay.

Damn. Instead, he'd done the opposite.

Well, they'd just have to manage. There were some things he couldn't do, even for his sons, and marrying was one of them.

"Do you like cooking, Leslie?" Justin asked. Once she had returned from the bunkhouse, the boys had attached themselves to her side.

"Why, yes, sweetie, I do. Why do you ask?"

"'Cause you was humming a song. Agnes wouldn't even let us stay in the kitchen with her, and she was always frowning."

"Maybe she was tired," Leslie suggested diplomatically. The more she heard about Agnes, however, the less she thought she'd been good for the boys.

"Leslie, do you have any kids?" Gareth asked, resting his chin in one palm as he watched her.

"No," she told him as she lifted the piecrust she'd been rolling out onto a pie plate. She shot a quick glance at the boys and then looked away. She sure was enjoying her time with these two kids.

"Don't you want any?" Justin chimed in, moving to get on his knees in the chair with his brother and lean against the cabinet.

"Well, someday. I have to find a husband first."

"Why?"

That question stopped Leslie. She shot a quick look at the concentration on the boys' faces and hid her smile. "Because that's how you do it. First you get married and then you have kids." At least that was the way people *should* do it.

Before they could ask any more questions, she gathered the scraps of leftover piecrust. "Now it's your turn to cook."

She taught them to butter the dough, sprinkle it with sugar and cinnamon and put it in the oven.

"Does it taste good?" Gareth asked, his gaze glued to the pan.

"Sure does. My mother used to help me make them when I was your age."

"She sounds like a great mama," Justin said with a sigh.

"Yes, she was."

"Isn't she your mama anymore?"

Leslie smiled at his serious little face. "She'll always be my mama, Justin, but she's dead now."

"Oh. So's our mama."

"Do you remember her?" Leslie asked, even though she felt guilty about doing so. She knew their father wouldn't like her asking questions.

Both boys shook their heads no.

"We was little babies."

The buzzer on the oven halted their conversation and for the next few minutes both boys were more interested in eating the pie dough treats with a glass of milk.

"There's only three left, Leslie. Do you want one?" Justin asked.

"No, thanks."

"What are you making now?"

"A chicken casserole that can be frozen for dinner tomorrow night." Concentrating on her cooking, Leslie didn't notice the silence for several minutes. When she did, she turned to observe her audience, only to find the two of them whispering.

"Is anything wrong?"

"We was wonderin', Leslie, if we could take these three pieces to Daddy?" Justin asked. "He would like them."

She checked her watch. It was a little after three. He might be waking up from the last dose of medication. "That's very thoughtful of you, boys. If you'll be careful, you can take some milk up, too."

"Aren't you coming with us?"

"No. I'm sure you can manage on your own." Truth was, she had no intention of going to that man's bedroom ever again. Every time she did, all she could think about was how it felt to be pressed against his long body.

The boys climbed the stairs carefully. When they pushed open the door, they discovered their father lying in bed, his eyes open.

"We brought you another treat, Daddy," Justin said. "Leslie makes the best treats! And we helped."

"Great. Uh, boys, don't jiggle the bed," he added with a grimace. "Where's Leslie?" he asked when she didn't appear behind the boys.

"She said we could manage. And we did!" Justin assured him, beaming.

"Want us to fix the pillows again?" Gareth asked, already running around the bed to grab the other pillow.

"Uh, yeah," their father muttered, slowly shifting himself to a sitting position. What was she trying to pull, sending the boys up alone? Okay, so he'd been rude. He'd apologize if she'd come back.

"Thanks, guys. This looks— Milk?" he questioned as Justin handed him a glass.

"Don't you like milk, Daddy? We drank it with ours."

"Uh, okay, sure. I just thought— I usually have coffee," he added. "But milk is fine."

The boys' anxious looks turned to grins when a sigh of pleasure escaped their father's lips. "It's good, isn't it?" Justin prodded.

"Pure ambrosia," he replied.

"No, Daddy," Gareth insisted, "it's pie dough. Leslie said."

"Daddy, we want Leslie to stay," Gareth added, ready to get to the heart of the matter. "She cooks real good."

"I know she does, boys, but—but there are other things to consider."

"She's pretty," Justin said earnestly, "and she sings while she cooks."

"And you shouldn't fight with her," Gareth added.

"Look, guys, things are a little more complicated than you realize." He sighed as his boys stared at him, waiting. "Okay, I shouldn't have gotten angry with her. She's our guest. I won't upset her anymore."

Uninvited guest, but guest all the same.

"She *likes* cooking," Justin insisted.

"And she lets us help her... and stay in the kitchen with her. Agnes always wanted us to go away and leave her alone," Gareth explained.

Doug frowned. "She sent you away? What did you do?"

"We watched cartoons a lot. And sometimes we made things," Gareth said, hanging his head. "That's when we always got in trouble."

"I see." And he did. Doug felt like the worst father in the world. He'd assumed, because Agnes was a decent cook and a woman, that she'd take good care of his boys. He should have paid more attention to what was going on. "Sorry, guys. Looks like I should've found someone better to take care of you."

"It's okay, Daddy," Justin assured his father. "We've got Leslie now."

"Justin, Leslie isn't going to stay. She's—she's just passing through."

"Passing through what?"

"I mean, she'll have to go back home."

"Why?"

"Yeah, why, Daddy?" Gareth chimed in.

"Because she doesn't live here."

"But she don't got no children. And she likes us!" Gareth assured him, making that in itself sound like a miracle.

Doug felt a little flustered, unable to explain why the beautiful woman downstairs couldn't stay. But he knew she couldn't. If for no other reason, because she was too much of a temptation.

The telephone ringing gave him some relief. He picked up the receiver beside his bed at the same time Leslie answered downstairs.

"Hello, Graybow Ranch."

"Who's speaking?"

"Leslie Hibbets."

"Miss Hibbets, this is Dr. Kelsey, Doug's doctor. I just wanted to see how he was doing."

"I believe he's fine, Dr. Kelsey, other than sleeping a lot. We've been giving him the pain pills every four hours. He's awake now if you'd like to talk to him."

"Yes, I would."

"I'm here, Jim," Doug said, knowing he should've acknowledged his presence earlier. A gasp and the immediate hanging up of the downstairs receiver told him Leslie thought so, too.

"How are you feeling, Doug? How's the headache?"

"Much better, thanks, Jim."

"Good. Uh, was that the lady you were worried about?"

Doug sighed. He knew he'd have to answer questions. "Yeah."

"She's staying to take care of you and the boys?"

"Just for a day or two. Until Moss can find someone else." His voice grew self-conscious as he muttered Moss's preposterous lie. "You know of anyone who's available? It won't be that long until I'm up and around with a cast, will it?"

"Nope, but I don't know of anyone. We're short-handed here at the hospital as it is. You'd better hang on to the sweet-voiced woman you've got. Or if you don't want her, send her over to me." Jim's voice carried the same reaction Moss had exhibited that morning. Doug was sick and tired of Leslie charming everyone she came into contact with. Except him, of course.

"I don't think she'd be interested."

"Well, be sure to stay in bed until Friday. I'll expect you back here early that morning so I can get a cast on your leg. And call if there are any problems, okay?"

"Yeah."

"Oh, and Doug?"

"Yeah?"

"When you can't change something, you might as well lay back and enjoy it."

Doug hung up without saying goodbye. He didn't need any more advice about the lady downstairs.

LESLIE WATCHED with a pleased smile as the aroma of the beef stew reached the cowboys when they piled inside the warmth of the bunkhouse. Their eagerness and appreciation made up for Doug Graybow's dislike.

As soon as she could, Leslie voiced the question that had been in her head all day. "Uh, Moss? Have you thought of anyone who could take my place?"

She noted that the other men looked as anxiously at Moss as she did.

"Well, no, Leslie, I haven't. I figured I'd make a few calls this evening. Ask a few of the ladies, you know? And see if I can find anyone. Uh, could you possibly stay a few more days if I don't find anyone? I mean, I know it's an inconvenience, but..." He let his voice trail off and pleaded with her with his eyes.

"Moss, I told you *I* wasn't the problem." Leslie knew what the cowhand was doing, but she couldn't be a part of it. Doug Graybow had made his feelings too clear.

"Then what *is* the problem?" one of the cowboys asked Moss.

"I'll explain later," he muttered before turning back to Leslie. "You go on up to the house and feed those young 'uns and I'll be along later to talk to the boss."

Leslie shrugged and closed the dishwasher. "Okay. But be as quick as you can. I need to go back to the motel tonight."

Moss frowned but only nodded.

She returned to the house and prepared a tray for the ornery man upstairs. When she nudged the door open, she stood on the threshold watching the three males without speaking. Doug was in the center of his big bed, the pillows piled behind him, and the two boys were flanking him, a head on each shoulder, as he read a story to them.

"And the Power Rangers—"

The aroma of the stew must have alerted him to her presence, because Doug looked up and stopped as his gaze met hers.

"Sorry to interrupt. I brought up your dinner."

"It smells great."

"Moss said he'd be up as soon as they finish eating. I'll leave as soon as he gets here." She ignored the boys' protests and sent them to wash for dinner.

Without waiting for him to comment on her announcement, she followed the boys out the door, leaving Doug to eat his dinner. And feel miserable.

AFTER EATING EVERY SPECK of food she'd left for him, in spite of his worries, Doug slid the tray to the floor and leaned back against the pillows. He was feeling much better, his head almost clear and his leg not bothering him unless he had to move.

So what was he going to do now?

He'd slept most of the day. He couldn't move. He had no television in his room. A book? He enjoyed murder mysteries in his few moments of relaxation, but he didn't have any on hand he hadn't read.

The sound of laughter from downstairs only emphasized his loneliness. Of course, his children would come back upstairs if he called them, but somehow he didn't think he had enough energy to entertain them tonight.

When he heard the sound of Moss's voice mixing with those of his children and Leslie, he cheered up. Moss would be up to visit with him. That would help pass the time.

Fifteen minutes later, Doug was fuming. It appeared Leslie's charms were more interesting to Moss than his boss's welfare. Just as he was building up enough anger to shout the house down, he heard the heavy tread of Moss's boots on the stairway.

"Howdy, boss," the cowboy said with a grin as he entered.

"I'm glad you could work me into your schedule," Doug ground out and then regretted his hasty words.

Moss's eyebrows rose but he said nothing.

"How did the day's work go?" Doug hurriedly asked, hoping his foreman would forget his petulant comment.

"Just fine. We counted and I don't think we lost a single cow or calf. And the weather report for tomorrow looks good."

"Great. Just great." Doug shifted in the bed, still embarrassed by his idiotic remark.

"That don't mean we don't have problems, though."

Doug's gaze snapped back to Moss's face, concern filling him. "What is it? Some disease? Is someone hurt?"

"Naw, nothing like that. But all the boys voted to quit if Leslie don't stay."

Chapter Five

Doug's mouth dropped open and he stared at Moss. "What did you say?" he finally asked.

"The boys say they'll walk out if you send Leslie away." Moss sounded like he was discussing the weather instead of threatening to close down Doug's ranch.

"You're joking."

"Did you eat her apple pie? Have a bowl of stew? Nope, I'm not jokin'."

"Moss, the men wouldn't walk away from a good job because someone who fixed them a decent meal was let go," Doug protested. "Besides, we can't force her to stay. She's already said she's leaving."

Moss hooked one work-worn boot around the bottom of the nearest chair and dragged it over to the bed. "See, it's this way, boss. I had to tell the boys that Leslie will stay, but you want her to go. Which means we'll be back to cold sandwiches after working all day, and one of us will have to ride herd on you and those two tornadoes you call your sons."

"They've been real good lately," Doug protested.

"Yeah, ever since Leslie arrived."

Doug couldn't argue with that statement. Nor could he promise better meals when they were already short-handed and would be more so now. He needed Blackie in the saddle instead of in the kitchen.

"Look, Moss, we'll work something out..." Doug began but trailed off at the stubborn look on his fore-man's face.

"Oh, yeah? What? Did you try to find anyone to-day?"

Doug reluctantly nodded.

"And?"

"There wasn't anyone."

"So what have you got against Leslie? She's per-fect."

Doug shot a disgusted look at Moss. "You know what I've got against Leslie. She came here because of that blasted ad! I have no intention of marrying again, even for my boys, and certainly not to satisfy my men's appetites!"

Moss muttered something about appetites, but Doug didn't want to know what he was saying. Finally Moss added, "Well, couldn't you make it clear that you're talking about a temporary thing? Just a job? I mean, she don't seem to be pining away for you."

Doug stiffened. That was all he needed, for his fore-man to insult his sex appeal while he lay flat on his back, feeling useless. Not that he wanted to appeal to Leslie Hibbets.

"I don't think she'd be interested in working as my housekeeper," he snapped.

"Hellfire, man! You're the stubbornest cuss I've ever seen. Would you just ask her?" Moss shook his head in disgust.

"I can't. She's mad at me. She said she was leaving as soon as you got here."

"And you're just lettin' her go?" Moss demanded, jumping up from his chair. Before he could leave, Doug supposed with the intention of stopping Leslie, the door was slammed back against the wall.

"Don't you think you've gone beyond the limit, Mr. Graybow?" a trembling Leslie demanded, her hands on her hips.

"Good evening to you, too," he muttered, trying not to watch as her chest rose up and down with her anger.

"I was willing to help out until you could find someone else, until you insulted me, that is. Sabotage wasn't necessary!" she raged on.

"Leslie, what are you talkin' about?" Moss demanded.

"Just go look! I can't believe—"

"*I* can't go look, so tell me what brought on this tantrum!" Doug insisted, irritation growing.

"Tantrum? When I took my bag to the car, I discovered my back tire flat."

"You're blaming me for a flat tire? I can't even get out of bed without crutches!"

The storm in her dissipated somewhat as his words sank in. "But maybe you asked someone to—"

"Tires go flat all the time. It's just bad timing. You shouldn't blame someone else for your misfortune." He regretted those words as soon as they came out. She wasn't slow to jump on them, either.

"Misfortune? Like falling in the snow?"

Doug took her meaning at once. With a sigh, he said, "I apologize for my earlier remarks. They were—were uncalled-for." There. He'd gotten out his apology. Which he would've made sooner if she hadn't avoided him.

"Thank you."

"Well? Aren't you going to apologize for suspecting me of making your tire go flat?"

"I would, if I thought it being sawed in half could be explained any other way." She'd crossed her arms over her chest, drawing Doug's attention to her anatomy once more. He barely took in her words until Moss choked.

"What did you say?"

When she opened her mouth to repeat her outrageous remark, he held up his hand. "Never mind. Moss, would you see if it's true, and if it is, round up you-know-who when you come back."

He could tell his orders to Moss irritated her, but he didn't care. Just as he heard Moss returning, she thought to question the last of his words.

"What did you mean about—"

"Boys!" Moss roared behind them. "In your dad's room on the double!"

She whirled around to stare at the door and then faced Doug again. "Surely you don't suspect the boys of doing such a thing? That's ridiculous."

"Who else would you like to blame? I'm stuck in bed and the cowboys were in the saddle."

"But surely they wouldn't—"

Moss and the twins halted her protest.

"Here are the terrible twins," Moss announced dryly.

"Boys, do you have something to confess?" Doug looked at his children sternly.

The two boys exchanged a glance and then turned to Leslie, tears in their eyes. "We didn't want you to go, Leslie. We *need* you!" Justin pleaded.

"Can't you stay?" Gareth added.

"You really did that to my tire?" she asked.

"And your spare," Moss added.

"But how?"

The twins ducked their heads. At last, after a growl from their father, Justin admitted, "While you went to the bunkhouse. We got the saw they use on the trees 'cause it has two handles."

"And we borrowed your keys so we could fix the other tire, too. But we put your keys back in your purse," Gareth added, a hopeful expression on his face.

"Boys, that was wrong. You must apologize to Leslie," Doug insisted.

"Okay, but will you stay?"

Leslie stared at the boys, a fascinated look on her face. Finally, she said, "I think that discussion must be between your father and me. But I certainly couldn't stay if I thought such terrible behavior would happen again."

Doug watched as his two boys wrapped their arms around Leslie's long legs, promising feverishly never to be so bad again. He'd certainly never received that response before.

Leslie looked at him and then Moss, as if waiting for something.

"Uh, boys, go to your room and think about what you've done. I'll let you know your punishment later." With a few pitiful sniffs and pleading looks toward Leslie, the boys shuffled out of the room. "And close your door, too," Doug added, knowing they'd be trying to overhear the adult conversation.

"I'll just wait downstairs in the kitchen," Moss said hurriedly. "Remember what we said, though, Doug," he added before rushing out the door.

After an awkward silence, Doug cleared his throat. "Well, I apologize for my children. And, of course, I'll buy you a new tire and a spare."

"Thank you."

Whew. She wasn't going to be a pushover. He cleared his throat again.

"Look, Leslie, we kind of got off to a bad start. I—I can't offer you what you want, even though you'd be—be great if that was—" He was beginning to sweat.

"I realize you have no interest in me." Her words were frigid.

"It's not, that is, I—" Hell, how did he get out of this fix? "I could use some temporary help," he said in a rush. Might as well lay his cards on the table. "*Temporary,*" he repeated, in case she missed the word the first time. "You know, just some housekeeping."

She looked startled. Well, housekeeping wasn't the top of most young women's career lists, he supposed. But it would solve almost all of his problems if she'd agree.

Leslie stared at the man stretched out on the bed. Two days ago, she would've been thrilled at his offer. Now she hesitated. Not because of the twins, though they were certainly unpredictable.

No, it was their father who made her hesitate. There was an attraction she'd felt from the first and she was afraid he'd break her heart.

"Temporary, for how long?" she finally asked.

"Until Friday at least. Maybe until after Christmas. My cast will be off by New Year's."

"I could stay until New Year's if you're sure you want me to." She almost held her breath waiting for his answer.

"It would help a lot. You'd have to take care of the twins, too. I know what they did was bad, but—"

"It's all right. But I believe they should have to work for the price of the tires. I don't want them to think their handiwork is why I'm staying."

"No, of course not, but I don't know—"

"I'll give them chores." She suddenly blushed, afraid she'd overstepped the limits of her new position. "I mean, they're your children, but if I'm going to take care of them, I must have your backing."

"Of course," he immediately agreed.

"I'm not trying to act like their mother, just their— their baby-sitter."

Her words put Doug in a panic all over again. Did she understand that he wasn't considering marriage? "Right. Their *temporary* baby-sitter."

When she only nodded, he called to Moss. His foreman appeared in the doorway almost instantly and Doug wondered if he'd been listening outside the door. "Uh, Leslie has agreed to stay until New Year's to help out. Would you go to Riverside and get her a couple of tires?"

"I need to go, too, and pick up my other bag from the motel."

"I'll take care of that for you," Moss assured her and was out the door before she could say anything.

"But I didn't give him any money," she protested.

"I'll take it out of your wages," Doug said, smiling slightly. He wanted to be sure she understood he was paying her. Nothing personal was involved.

"WE FINISHED OUR JOB, Leslie," Gareth said importantly. Justin was silent but he slipped his small hand into hers and squeezed it.

"That's great, boys." She'd given the boys their first task, folding some towels, as part of their punishment.

"Why don't I go run your bathwater." She took Gareth's hand, also, and began leading them up the stairs. "Afterward, the first Christmas special is coming on television. Would you like to watch it with me?"

"You're not mad at us?" Justin asked timidly, and Leslie tried not to smile. They were rascals, these two, but charmers all the same.

"No, of course not, though what you did was wrong." She frowned at both of them for emphasis. "Now, let's hurry so we won't miss the start of the program."

"Hey, yeah. Will we see Santa? And a pretty Christmas tree?" Justin asked, jumping up and down.

"Probably."

"We don't ever have a Christmas tree," Gareth said in his most dramatic voice, a hangdog look on his face.

In spite of the child's obvious hamming, what he said stopped Leslie cold. "What did you say?" she asked, halting just outside their father's room.

"We don't ever have a Christmas tree. Daddy don't have time and Agnes don't like them. She says they're messy and too much trouble."

Leslie turned to stare in disbelief, anger and outrage at Doug Graybow. How could he treat his own children like that? Her own past overflowed with such wonderful memories of Christmas, she couldn't imagine her childhood without it. Suddenly she was very glad she'd agreed to stay.

"Is that true, Doug?" she asked as the man lay watching them.

He shifted on the mattress, making her all too aware of his lean body. "I don't do much celebrating at Christmas," he said with a shrug.

Kneeling down with an arm around each boy, she said, "Your daddy asked me to stay until his leg is all better, and I said yes. That means I'll be here until after Christmas. So this year you're going to have a Christmas tree. The best Christmas tree ever. Okay?"

The boys jumped and cheered, hugging her neck and offering suggestions for the tree. After a minute or two, Leslie sent them on their way to the tub for their bath, promising to be there in a minute to run their bathwater.

As soon as the boys were gone, she moved to Doug's door. "I agreed to stay to help out, Mr. Douglas Graybow. But now I'm staying for another reason. I'm going to make this the best Christmas ever for your children. How could you deny them the joy of Christmas? That's cruel."

With that, she slammed the door, not even waiting for his response.

GREAT! First the woman thought he'd tried to paw her. Now she believed him worse than Scrooge. He'd better make sure she didn't meet his neighbors while she was here, or she'd smash his reputation to pieces.

Doug sank back against the pillows with a groan. It wasn't as if he ignored Christmas. The boys always had presents to open. He never forgot to give Agnes some money to go into town and buy whatever she thought the boys would like. But the ideas of decorating a tree and singing carols and things like that were too tiring for him to organize after a long day in the saddle.

He remembered the Christmas magic his own mother had created. The stocking she'd made for him, her Christmas baking that had filled the air, the church service on Christmas Eve she'd always insisted they attend—all those had played a part in his childhood. He particularly remembered the special ornaments they'd used to decorate the tree.

Since his parents' death, he'd never even taken the ornaments from the attic. The first Christmas after his marriage, life had been too chaotic. The twins were only six weeks old and Bettina wasn't adapting well to motherhood. Agnes had had her hands full with mother and babies. The next Christmas, the twins were still little and he and Bettina were so at odds, they'd hardly spoken to each other, much less wanted to share Christmas. Before the next Christmas, he was a widower and he'd wanted to avoid the realities of his life.

But he should have remembered his sons. After all, he was responsible for them. And he did love them. He'd just forgotten to care for them.

Damn Leslie Hibbets! She always made him feel inadequate. Next, she'd be telling him he should remarry for the sake of his kids. Then she'd suggest herself, and they'd be right back to square one.

Well, no way! He'd been trapped into marriage once. It wouldn't happen again.

The sound of childish giggles floated down the hallway. There'd been a lot more of such happy sounds since Leslie Hibbets arrived, he'd have to admit. So, okay, she could have her Christmas tree. And anything else she thought up. He'd cooperate, which would probably send her into shock.

For his boys he'd help make it a Merry Christmas. But then she was out the door.

He wasn't getting trapped again.

LESLIE TUCKED IN the boys with promises of Christmas plans they'd made while they watched the television program. Gareth wanted real candy canes on the tree, and Justin thought icicles were the most beautiful things he'd ever seen.

She'd assured them they could both have their wishes.

Unless Scrooge intervened.

"Humph!" *Just let him try. I'll show him.*

"Leslie?"

The sound of the tyrant's voice intruded on her thoughts. She was tempted to walk right past his room. But she couldn't be that rude.

"Yes, Mr. Graybow?" she replied stiffly, standing in the doorway of his bedroom.

He heaved a sigh, and she was reminded of Gareth. Some of the child's dramatic bent must've come from his father.

"Has Moss returned?"

"No."

"Oh."

"Is there anything else?" she asked even as she took a step back into the hallway.

"Yes, damn it!"

His sudden burst of impatience halted her retreat. "Yes?"

"I'm bored to tears. There's nothing to read, the television is downstairs and I've done all the thumb twiddling I can stand."

She'd thought herself hardened to his situation, because of his desire to be rid of her and her anger about Christmas, but the years of tending her mother, who'd assured her that boredom was the biggest burden of all, made it impossible to walk away.

"When Moss comes back, I'll ask him to move the television up here," she suggested.

"That would help," he agreed with a weary sigh.

"In the meantime, do you have a deck of cards? Would you like to play?"

He appeared surprised by her offer, and she expected him to refuse. After all, he'd made his dislike of her company obvious. Instead, however, he grinned like a little boy opening a wonderful present. "Gin?" he asked, his brown eyes sparkling.

"Are you any good?" she returned, determined to keep him at a distance. Somehow, just being in his bedroom immediately brought back the memory of removing his jeans.

"Good enough," he drawled, a challenge in his voice.

"Where are the cards?" She'd spent a lot of years playing cards with her mother. Mr. Douglas Graybow was in for a surprise.

She found the deck of cards and settled down in a chair beside the bed. At first, she kept her gaze steadily on her cards, but gradually, with his good humor, she relaxed and found herself watching him.

When he was in a good mood, his charm was overpowering, particularly when combined with his good looks. His long frame beneath the covers caused her some real distraction. But she won the first hand.

Doug covertly watched Leslie consider her cards. Her blue eyes peeked at him over the top of them, and he couldn't help smiling at her. She'd entertained and teased him, once she relaxed, and he'd enjoyed himself. Even though he'd had to struggle with his physical reaction to her.

Somehow, the floral scent she wore seemed to encircle him, but he was comfortable with it. As if he'd been closer. And he wished he could be. Without any complications, of course.

He didn't want a wife, a long-term commitment. But a little feminine company could be a good thing. As long as there were rules and everyone understood it was temporary. She leaned forward to draw a card, and Doug almost rolled off the bed as he responded. *Get control of yourself, man!*

"Are you all right?" Leslie asked, looking up from her cards.

"Sure. Just lost my balance."

"Oh, sorry. Gin!"

She sure knew how to distract a guy.

When Moss arrived half an hour later, he appeared shocked to find his boss and the housekeeper deeply involved in a game of cards.

"Am I interrupting?"

"Yeah," Doug growled, staring at the cards in his hand.

"Did you bring my bag?" Leslie asked, unconcerned with Doug's concentration.

Doug discarded the one card she needed for gin. Without any gloating, she picked the card up, selected another and discarded it facedown. "Gin."

"Damn it, Les! I think you're cheating," Doug challenged, but there was a teasing glint in his eyes that made Leslie catch her breath.

"Now, boss, that's not gentlemanly," Moss said.

"You can't worry about being a gentleman in a cutthroat game like this one. She's going to break me."

"That's right, that's my plan," she assured him. "I won that game by fifty-six points."

"What are you playin' for?" Moss asked.

"A penny a point," she assured him with a superior smile intended to nudge Doug's pride. "I'm going to save my winnings and buy the ranch out from under him.''

''How much have you won so far?''

''Eighty-three cents.'' She leaned toward Moss and asked in a hushed voice, as if Doug couldn't hear, ''Do you think he's good for it?''

''Don't get too cocky, young lady,'' Doug warned, but there was laughter in his voice.

''Cocky? I'm basing my expectations on skill, I'll have you know.'' She stood and looked at Moss. ''Would you like me to leave so the two of you can talk?''

''Naw, it's past my bedtime. You two go ahead with your game.'' He gave a wave and hurried back down the stairs.

''Are you ready to call it a night?'' Leslie asked, as if she suddenly became aware of their isolation.

''No, I need to win back my money.''

The smile that took his breath away lit her face again. ''Wishful thinking,'' she warned him with a raised eyebrow before she sat back down and shuffled the deck.

He was all too aware of that.

Chapter Six

Doug shivered, suddenly realizing he was astride Diamond, his favorite mount, in a snowstorm, wearing his navy dress suit. Why was he dressed for church?

As if that thought had made it appear, the steeple of the small church he attended became visible in the snowstorm. There were a lot of cars parked around it, and light streamed out into the storm from its windows.

Fear turned his stomach into a churning frenzy. Had someone died? Where were his boys? Why was he alone? Suddenly he was at the steps of the church and someone reached out to take the reins from him. He slid from Diamond's back and approached the door.

To his relief, Justin and Gareth appeared at his side, each taking a cold hand. He felt calmer, happier, relieved to see the gay atmosphere of the church, dressed in Christmas finery. He turned to smile at a neighbor when he noticed the white flowers lining the aisle, the white runner . . .

A wedding?

He stared down the aisle that appeared miles long. Yet he could clearly see Leslie's beautiful face, her chestnut hair unbraided, spread across her shoulders, under the bridal veil.

Eagerly he started down the aisle. Leslie. He was no longer cold. Now he was burning, eager to reach her, to toast himself on the warmth of her smile. His boys were chanting as they kept pace with him. Something about a mother.

The people in the church were cheering. The pastor waited at the altar beside his bride. He finally reached the end of the long aisle and reached out to take her hands. The minister began the vows, but the fear returned.

Slowly, with shaking hands, he lifted the veil—and it was Bettina, a spiteful look on her face. He gasped and backed away as she began laughing hysterically.

"No—no, no!"

"Here now, I thought you wanted this television up here. That's what Leslie said."

Doug jackknifed in the bed, staring at Moss. The foreman was holding the television at the foot of his bed.

"Are you all right, Doug?"

"I—I was asleep," he told Moss even as he stared at his surroundings to be sure.

Moss set down the television and stepped back to the door. "Leslie? You'd better come check on Doug."

"No!" Doug protested, but it was too late. He could hear Leslie's light step on the stairs. Only seconds later, she appeared in the doorway.

With a groan, he flopped back onto his pillow and closed his eyes. She was wearing white.

"What's wrong?"

"Doug said he was sleepin', but he's sweatin' somethin' fierce."

Doug's eyes popped back open when he felt Leslie's cool hand on his brow. She was bent over the bed, offering a tempting glimpse of shadowy cleavage that didn't stop his sweating. Her perfume surrounded him.

"Doug? How are you feeling?"

A thousand violins couldn't sound so heavenly, he thought dreamily, then yanked himself back to reality. "Fine!" he said roughly and turned his face away.

"I think he must still have a headache. I probably shouldn't have let him play cards so long last night," she confided to Moss.

"I'm not dead yet!" Doug snapped. "Don't talk as if I can't hear you."

Leslie lifted one brow as a comment on his mulish behavior and turned away. When she'd left the room, Moss grinned at him. "You sure are lucky she's a patient lady, or you would've lost your head already."

Doug knew he shouldn't have been so rude, but he'd panicked. Last night had been too enjoyable. Leslie had been too tempting.

Blast it! He was not going to fall into that trap again! A pretty face, along with a beguiling smile and curves in all the right places, was not going to lead him astray. He'd promised himself he'd avoid marrying again at all costs.

Bettina had been pretty. Since she and her parents had just moved to the area, she was the hot number everyone sought. He'd lusted after her along with the rest of the local guys. When she'd selected him to date, he'd been as proud as he could be.

Three months later, she informed him she was pregnant and expected him to do the right thing. He had. But after the marriage ceremony, he discovered there was more to Bettina than beauty. She was spoiled, selfish and silly. He'd tried to be a good husband, but running a ranch wasn't an easy job. Bettina wanted to be waited upon; she didn't want to put forth any effort herself.

Even so, he'd tried. That's when he'd hired Agnes to work for them. That move had placated Bettina for a while. Until after the babies were born. She'd been furious with him because she'd had twins, as if he'd created two boys on purpose. When he complained because she always wanted to go to town, never spending any time with their babies, she'd informed him she wasn't interested in children.

After all, she'd said, she'd only gotten pregnant so he'd marry her.

"Is this place okay?" Moss asked, snapping him from his painful memories.

"Yeah. Fine." He had other things to worry about besides where Moss put the television.

"Are you sure you still want it? You seem kind of undecided this morning."

"That'll be fine for now. I won't need it after Friday. But I'm going crazy with nothing to do."

"You've got Leslie to entertain you," Moss suggested with a sly grin.

The fear returned. "Just connect the television, Moss."

Moss quickly followed his orders before heading for the barn. Doug wished he could go with him.

Especially when he heard Leslie's soft footsteps coming toward him. He tensed, waiting for her to appear.

"I brought you some more of your medicine to take with your breakfast."

He stared at her, unable to forget the image of her waiting at the end of the aisle, beautiful in her white gown. Was it just coincidence that she had a white sweater on this morning, some kind of crocheted thing that made a man think he might be seeing more than he should?

"Doug? Doug? Are you all right? Should I call the doctor?"

"No!" he answered sharply. He just needed to be left in peace. Alone.

"Fine," she said coolly and left the room. He must've spoken the words he'd thought.

Loneliness engulfed him.

OF ALL THE ORNERY, contrary, difficult men, Doug Graybow was the worst.

Last night, she'd almost forgotten his desire to be rid of her as they'd matched wits over the card game. He'd teased her and harangued her when she won, but always nicely. The companionship had been wonderful.

But things had changed overnight.

And it was just as well. She'd warned herself not to start thinking about Doug Graybow as a man.

"Have you finished your pancakes?" she asked the twins as she entered the kitchen.

"Yeah, Leslie. They were great!" Gareth exclaimed.

"Yeah!" echoed Justin.

"Good. Take your plates to the dishwasher."

Even though both boys obeyed, she noticed a slacking of enthusiasm in them. "Anything wrong?"

"We never had to do things like this when Agnes was here," Gareth explained. "If you're our housekeeper, why don't you do it?"

Kneeling down in front of the boys, she said, "There are several reasons. Put your dishes away and then I'll explain."

The thought of something new perked up their interest and they did as she requested. Seated between them at the table, she said, "First of all, you are going to do extra chores in payment for my tires. You haven't forgotten, have you?"

The boys hung their heads and indicated their memory was still intact.

"Good. But even if you weren't being punished, you'd have to do chores. You see, a housekeeper is hired to do the laundry, cook the meals and clean the house. I'm also supposed to take care of the two of you."

"Well, isn't that taking care of us?"

"Yes, Gareth, it is. But it isn't the best thing for you."

"Why not?" Justin asked.

"Because I won't always be here. And even if I were going to be here forever, you might not. You'll need to know how to take care of yourselves. I'm going to teach you how to do laundry, how to clean and how to cook. Then I know you'll be able to take care of yourselves when I go."

"We don't want you to go," Justin protested, reaching out to touch her.

Leslie dropped a kiss on his frown and smiled. "I'm very glad to hear it." At least *someone* wanted her here.

"Now, I want you to go upstairs to your dad's room. 'Sesame Street' is just about to start. Every morning, I want you to watch that program and 'Mr. Rogers.'"

"We've never seen those shows," Justin said.

Leslie rolled her eyes. Why hadn't Agnes let the boys watch them? No wonder the twins were always into mischief. "You'll like them."

She led the two boys upstairs as she practiced what she was going to say to her grumpy employer. The hour and a half the boys were learning would give her a chance to organize her job and start work. If Mr. Douglas Graybow allowed them to watch the television.

The door was closed and she rapped on it.

"Yes?"

Opening the door, she shepherded the boys in front of her. Doug was under the covers, the tray filled with empty dishes beside him.

"I wanted the boys to watch some educational programming while I get started working, if that's all right."

"Educational programming?"

" 'Sesame Street' and 'Mr. Rogers.' Have you heard of them?"

"Of course I have," he snapped.

"Good. Then I'm sure you understand how well they will prepare the boys for school."

"And leave you free to do what you want?"

His snarled question, more an accusation, made her angry. She drew a deep breath before responding. "Yes, I'm planning on improving my tan in the backyard. Please don't disturb me!" Since the weather outside just barely topped freezing, she thought Doug would catch her sarcasm.

She crossed the room to the television and turned it to "Sesame Street."

"I'll bring you a snack when 'Mr. Rogers' starts," she told the boys and turned to leave the room without a word to her employer.

"Leslie."

He didn't sound friendly, as he had last night, but Doug also didn't sound angry.

"Yes?" She couldn't help but look at him.

"If I apologize, could I have a cup of coffee? I'll even watch the programs, too." A childlike grin danced on his face.

She had to press her lips together to hold back a smile. But she managed. Damn him, she thought. He couldn't turn on the charm and expect her to melt. No matter how much she wanted to, she wouldn't give him the satisfaction.

THE HOUR AND A HALF he'd spent with his kids proved more interesting than he'd expected. Not only were the programs good, but Doug had enjoyed his children's reactions to them.

It bothered him to realize that as much as he'd blamed Bettina for not spending time with the boys, he hadn't, either. Never mind that he had the excuse of the ranch. He still should have been making more of an effort to be with his kids.

Leslie came up when "Mr. Rogers" ended. "I'll take the boys downstairs now. Do you have everything you need?" she asked, interrupting his self-castigation.

"Yeah. I'm fine." He let his gaze follow her across the room. Somehow, when she was in the room, he didn't see anything or anyone else.

"Do you have the remote control?"

He nodded. "Thanks for taking such good care of my children, Leslie. I appreciate it."

She flashed him a frowning glance and then urged the children to the door. "No problem."

He didn't blame her for being confused. He was confused about the feelings that filled him whenever she entered his room. Pleasure and fear warred, making him either cold or meltingly warm, like last evening.

At least he was sure about one thing. She was good for his boys. Even if she wasn't good for him.

AFTER LESLIE HAD TUCKED them in and turned off the light, Justin whispered, "I'm glad Leslie stayed. I think she'll make a great mommy."

"I guess," Gareth said.

"You don't love her?"

"Yeah, but I'm tired of doing chores."

"Well, we did do bad when we cut her tires," Justin reminded him.

"I know. Hey! Maybe that's how we'll convince Daddy that Leslie should be our mommy." Gareth sat up in the shadowy darkness. "What if we try to help everyone? You know, do good things."

"Do you think it would work?"

"Daddy would like it. And we could tell him it's 'cause of Leslie." Enthusiasm was growing in Gareth's voice.

"Okay. Tomorrow we'll be good helpers."

"Santa will like it, too. Then maybe he'll give us Leslie for Christmas."

"Yeah!" Justin agreed. "But we'll have to get a bigger stocking. She won't fit in one of ours."

AFTER WAKING UP from a nap Thursday afternoon, Doug reached for his crutches. Time for another of those excruciating trips to the bathroom. He was glad he would be returning to the doctor tomorrow to get a walking cast. He'd gladly throw the crutches away.

When his hand only encountered air where he'd left those torture sticks, he really came awake. Twisting, he leaned over the side of the bed, thinking the crutches might have fallen on the floor, under the bed.

Not again, he groaned, when he didn't find them. He remembered the first time he'd needed the crutches, his argument with Leslie and the boys finally rescuing him. The past few days, he'd avoided all arguments, and, as far as possible, he'd avoided Leslie. She drew his gaze too much as it was.

It wasn't just her body, though he had no complaints about that. It was her laughter, her quick-wittedness, her patience. Her blue eyes, her— The crutches, he reminded himself. He needed to find his crutches.

His gaze searched the room, but he couldn't see them anywhere. After a lusty sigh, he roared, "Boys!"

No response.

He listened and was able to hear faint noises, indicating he wasn't in the house alone, but he didn't hear any steps in his direction. He called several more times, but there was no answer.

Finally, in desperation, he shouted, "Leslie?"

Just when he was about to give up, he heard her steps on the stairs.

"Did you call?" she asked, sticking her head around the door. Her voice was breathless, as if she'd been running.

"Yeah. Is everything okay?"

She rolled her eyes and moved into the doorway. "No, not exactly."

"What did the boys do this time?" he asked in resignation.

"They were trying to help," she hastily assured him.

"What's that on your jeans?" he asked, noticing what looked like soapsuds clinging to her shapely legs.

"Part of the problem. The boys put in a load of clothes to wash." She paused before adding with a weary grin, "They used an entire box of soap powder. The laundry room is covered with bubbles. We're mopping it up. That's why we didn't hear you. What do you need?"

"I need my crutches so I can, uh, go to the bathroom."

Her teeth sank into her bottom lip.

"Uh-oh. Why do I get the feeling we have another problem?" he muttered, watching her.

"Because we do. When the laundry fiasco occurred, the boys decided maybe they should confess their other good deed of the day. I'm going to have to help you to the bathroom."

"Why?" Her helping him wouldn't be a good idea. It would involve touching, and he thought touching would be a big mistake.

"Well, when the boys decided to turn over a new leaf and be helpful, they thought of you first."

"What did they do?"

"They heard you complaining about the crutches making your armpits sore, and they wanted to fix them."

When she paused again, he couldn't wait. "Just spit it out. What did those two do this time?"

With a grin, Leslie reached out the door and pulled in the two crutches. At least they had been crutches. Now they were a modified version, sawed off to make them the right height for a midget.

He sighed. "The saw again?"

"Yes," she agreed with a chuckle. "I've told them to never use it again without permission." When he didn't say anything, she added, "At least they were *trying* to be helpful."

"I appreciate that, but it makes life difficult for me. I've got to get to the bathroom."

She stepped over to the side of the bed. "Come on. I'll help you until tomorrow."

"I'm not exactly dressed for an excursion in mixed company," he muttered, his cheeks heating up.

Leslie wanted to tell him that she'd already seen whatever he could show her. But she didn't want to embarrass him. "Do you have a robe?"

"Yeah, maybe. Look in the back of my closet."

She'd gotten used to taking care of Doug's laundry and putting it away. Yet going through his closet in his presence seemed strangely intimate.

At the back of the closet, as he'd said, she found an Indian blanket bathrobe. When she pulled it out, it didn't look as if it had ever been worn.

"Don't you use it?"

"No. I usually dress as soon as I'm up."

She carried the robe to the bed and held it out for him to slip into. After he'd shrugged it on, he tied it at the waist and slid to the edge of the bed.

Leslie caught a glimpse of strong, muscled legs before he tugged the robe in place as determinedly as a maiden aunt would. She bent over to slide her arm under his and across his back.

"What are you doing?" he demanded, rearing back away from her.

"Helping you up," she said, surprised. "Isn't that what you wanted me to do?"

He looked away, his cheeks still flushed. "Uh, yeah."

She bent over again. "Ready?" she asked, balancing herself by placing her other hand on his chest. She could feel his heart thumping at a fast pace under her hand and knew hers was just as rapid.

"Yeah," he growled next to her ear, sending shivers down her. She pulled and he pushed off the bed to a standing position. The result had her plastered to his side, her arms around him.

"Um, which side should I be on, your good leg or the broken one?" she asked, breathing deeply to calm herself.

"The broken one, I think," he said after a moment.

She circled to his other side and again put an arm around his back. "Put your arm across my shoulders," she ordered when he just stood there.

He said nothing but his arm encircled her and they started across the room. Never had the ten necessary paces seemed so long. Leslie was completely conscious of his arm around her, her arm around him, their closeness.

When they finally reached the bathroom door, she turned toward him to reach the knob to open it. Without realizing it, she pressed her breast into his chest. His sharp intake of air told her he noticed it.

Blushing a bright red, she edged away from him. "Can you manage from here?"

"Yeah," he growled.

"Okay. I'll wait here for when you're ready to go back." She was disgusted that her voice sounded as if she'd just run a marathon.

When Doug was ready to leave the bathroom, he gave himself a pep talk about resisting certain chestnut-haired beauties. He wasn't going to be affected by her curves plastered against him. He wasn't going to have fantasies about pulling her down on the bed with him. Definitely not.

He opened the door to find Leslie leaning against the wall, patiently waiting. She slid her arm around him again, and he laid his across her shoulders. Turning to look at her, he realized she was the perfect height, her shoulders fitting under his arms. All he'd have to do to kiss her was tip up her stubborn little chin and lean down.

"Doug?" she called, distracting him from his fantasy. "Are you ready?"

"Uh, yeah," he assured her and pulled her closer against him. As they hobbled back across the room, he turned his head and buried his nose against her hair. The clean, flowery smell he always associated with Leslie was there.

He was so distracted by her closeness, he didn't even notice that they'd reached the bed. When she released him, he still clung to her but his balance was thrown off.

He fell to the bed, taking Leslie with him. She sprawled across him in a most satisfactory manner.

"Daddy, what are you and Leslie doing?" a little voice asked from the doorway.

Chapter Seven

"You sure you can manage, Leslie?" Moss asked after closing the door on Doug. Leslie could understand his concern. Doug's moods had been unpredictable the four days since he broke his leg. Then, yesterday, after the crutches incident, his black mood had been constant.

Leslie pulled on her gloves as she answered. "Of course I can. The boys and I have a lot of errands to run, so there's no need for you to make the trip, as well."

"But he'll be cranky by the time you get him back here."

Leslie peered around Moss's solid frame to discover Doug staring at her through the car window, impatience on his face.

"He's cranky all the time, Moss. We'll manage just fine." It wasn't true, of course. There had been moments when he'd been pleasant. They'd never experienced the camaraderie they'd shared the one night they'd played cards, but then that was probably for the best.

After reassuring Moss several more times and warning the boys they had to wear the seat belt in the front passenger seat they were sharing, Leslie began the drive into Riverside.

"What was Moss saying?" Doug growled from the back seat.

"He was warning me that you might get cranky by the end of the day," she said, smiling in the rearview mirror. Just as she'd expected, he glowered back at her.

"And what did you say?"

"That crankiness wasn't a stranger around here."

"Cute, Leslie, real cute." He sank back against the pillows she'd piled into the back seat for him.

"I think Leslie's beautiful," Justin said, beaming up at her.

"Me, too," Gareth added. The boys always stuck together.

When there was an obvious silence from the back seat, Gareth twisted under the restraints of the seat belt and asked, "Don't you, Daddy?"

"Yeah," he muttered and shut his eyes.

Leslie asked the boys a question about something they'd watched on television the night before with their father, hoping to distract them. And wanting to ignore the hurt she felt from Doug's less-than-enthusiastic response.

She had more important things to think about, anyway. The list of things she needed in town had grown over the past few days to include an expansion of her wardrobe. The four outfits she had with her were getting a little old.

"When will we have our tree, Leslie?" Justin asked for the hundredth time.

"We're going to look for decorations today. Then, on Sunday afternoon, if your father has time—or maybe we should ask Moss—"

"I'll have time!" Doug snapped from the back seat.

Leslie peeped in the rearview mirror to see his glare before returning her gaze to the road. "Well, we'll find a tree on the ranch and cut it down and bring it back to the house. Then we can decorate it that evening. After all, today is the first of December."

"Why did we have to wait until the first?" Gareth demanded.

"Because Thanksgiving is in November. Besides, the tree will die too soon if we put it up much earlier."

"I don't 'member Thanksgiving," Justin said with a frown.

She looked again in the rearview mirror but Doug didn't meet her gaze. "Um, Thanksgiving is when you usually have a turkey dinner and say thanks for all you've been given."

"You mean like presents?" Justin asked. "'Cause we didn't get no presents in November."

"No, I mean saying thanks for your nice home, for food to eat, for your health—things like that."

"For you!" Gareth exclaimed. "We could say thank-you for you."

"And your father. And your warm clothes, your toys, the food you have to eat," Leslie added.

"Yeah. Did we do that, Daddy?"

Doug cleared his throat. "Sort of. We'll talk about it later."

The boys seemed to realize their father didn't want to talk, so they turned back to Leslie and began discussing their plans for the longed-for Christmas tree. That topic wasn't exhausted until they reached Riverside.

Leaving the boys in the car with their father, Leslie went into the hospital emergency entrance to get a wheelchair and some men to lift Doug into it.

"Excuse me," she said to the nurse behind the counter. "I've brought Doug Graybow to have his leg put in a cast, but I'll need help bringing him in."

"You must be Leslie," a deep voice said behind her. She turned around to discover a tall man in a white jacket.

"Yes. Are you Dr. Kelsey?"

"Yes, I am. Nancy, send two men out to bring Doug in." The nurse hurried to follow his orders, leaving them alone. "Will you join me in a cup of coffee?"

"Thank you for the offer, but the twins are in the car." She smiled and turned back to the door.

"I'll walk out with you. How is my patient?"

"If I say he's a grouch, will you hold it against me?"

"No, not at all. He hasn't had any recurring headaches, has he?"

"If he has, he hasn't told me about them." And probably wouldn't, she realized. A moment of panic seized her. Could Doug still be in pain and refusing to say anything? She would feel the lowest of the low if his foul moods were attributable to his accident.

She anxiously searched Doug's face as they walked to the parking lot. The sight of him talking and laughing with his boys relieved her anxiety. No, he wasn't in pain. He was just a grouch.

Dr. Kelsey swung the back door open. "Hi, Doug. How are you doing?"

"Fine, except for the bedsores. I may sleep standing up from now on."

"You should have asked your beautiful nurse here for a massage. Then you might change your mind."

Leslie felt her cheeks flush at such a suggestion. She noticed Doug, too, was embarrassed by the doctor's words. Perhaps he'd decided, as she had, that touching should be avoided. Opening her door, she slipped into the driver's seat.

"Doc, that was uncalled for," Doug mumbled.

"Sorry, but that's how you relieve bedsores. Oh, here come the orderlies with the wheelchair." The doctor stepped back to allow the two burly men room to maneuver.

The twins had released the seat belt and were kneeling in the front seat. "Daddy, you get to ride in that?" Gareth demanded, envy in his voice as he saw the wheelchair.

"Wow, I bet that's fun," Justin added.

"No, it's not. Boys, I want you to be good for Leslie, okay?"

"Sure, Daddy. When we come back, will you get to go back home with us?" Justin asked, a frown on his face.

"Of course I will. And I'll be able to move around, go back to work."

He needn't make it sound like he was returning to the Promised Land, she thought resentfully. She'd done everything she could to make his stay in bed pleasant. Except give massages, she remembered, her cheeks flushing again.

"Leslie, here," Doug said, just before the men scooted him out of the car.

She instinctively held out her hand, wondering what he was giving her. When she looked, she discovered a money clip with numerous bills in it.

Sliding from the car, she stood in front of the chair as the men settled him in. "What is this for?"

"It's for your shopping."

"I'm not buying supplies for the ranch." She tried to hand the money clip back to him.

He shoved her hand away. "You're buying things for my boys. I pay for my children."

"I'm buying things for *my* Christmas tree. And I pay for *my* things," she said, with just as much emphasis.

"Leslie, you're being stubborn. I'm not paying you enough salary for you to go spending it all on my kids. Besides, you can pick them up a gift or two from me while you're shopping."

Realization dawned on her. "Is that how you handled Christmas in the past? Just shove a few dollars at an employee and your responsibility is ended?" She tossed the money clip in his lap and crossed her arms. "Well, no thanks, Mr. Graybow. I won't do your shopping for you. I'm giving Justin and Gareth *my* version of Christmas. Not yours!"

"WHEW!" one of the orderlies exclaimed as Leslie jumped in the car and drove out of the parking lot.

"Yeah," Doug muttered in agreement, his gaze never leaving the disappearing car.

"Does she still want to marry you? Because she didn't seem too friendly," Jim teased, knocking Doug on the shoulder.

"Don't you start. Moss has already pointed out how little she's interested in me. It's my boys she's fallen in love with." Even as he made that statement, Doug realized it was true. Leslie had accepted his rejection of her without a complaint. She was focused on his children. At least in that respect she was different from Bettina. Of course, Bettina hadn't even been interested in him once she'd trapped him into marriage and gotten access to his money.

When she'd wrapped her new car around a post in a snowstorm, he'd been sorry. But overwhelming relief had filled him more than anything else. He'd buried himself in running the ranch, a responsibility he'd had since his own parents' early death in a plane crash.

But he was beginning to realize that in doing so, he'd excluded the two most precious gifts he'd ever received—his children. He looked down at the money clip still lying in his lap.

Leslie was right. He'd delegated his responsibilities for his children in the past. Now that he'd spent time with them, enforced by his broken leg, he was beginning to realize how much he'd neglected them.

No longer. This Christmas would be different. He might not be able to give them a mother, as the entire world seemed to think he should do, but he could be a better father. Not even Leslie would be able to fault him this Christmas.

"I need to use the phone," he told Jim as the orderlies wheeled him into the hospital.

"You forget something?"

"Yeah, for about five years. But it's not too late. It wasn't for Scrooge and it isn't for me." His lips firmed in grim determination.

"I don't think it should be so painful," Jim chided softly.

"What?"

"You look like you've been visited by the Grim Reaper. I thought Leslie was the Christmas Angel. She should bring a smile to your lips. She certainly does to mine."

"Hey!" Doug protested, a twinge somewhere in his heart region disturbing him. "Leslie belongs to me!"

"To you?"

"I mean, to—to the Bar-G," he said, naming his spread. His head was whirling with what he'd just said.

He wanted no part of Leslie and her intentions, right? With a suppressed groan, he faced the truth he'd been avoiding. He didn't want to marry Leslie, or anyone for that matter, but he wanted her.

He wanted her in every way a man could want a woman, but one. He wanted to touch her, feel her pressed against him, as she had been yesterday when they fell to the bed. He wanted to hold her again, and not let her go until he'd satisfied both their hungers.

Because he wasn't the only one who felt anything. Leslie's flushed cheeks, the response he could feel in her, told him she had noticed the attraction that hummed between them.

But he couldn't do anything about that attraction. Because the price was too high. Leslie had come to marry him, not bed him. Damn. Jim's voice brought Doug back to the moment.

"Can't blame a guy for looking, Doug. Right, boys?" Jim asked the two orderlies, who grinned in return and nodded.

"She's a beauty, even if she does have a temper," one offered.

"And she did something I've never seen a woman do," the second said. "She turned down money."

"There you go, Doug. She's quite a woman. You'd better grab her before someone else does," Jim warned.

"Mind your own business," Doug snapped. The last thing he needed was advice from someone who didn't understand the situation. Who didn't recognize the trap that awaited him. A trap baited with a very desirable woman.

"You know, one other thing about Leslie..." Jim said, ignoring Doug's order.

Doug waited for whatever Jim might say, but when the doctor remained silent, he was forced to ask. "Well?"

"She said you were a grouch, and she was right."

LESLIE HAD PROMISED Dr. Kelsey she'd be back at three, but the shopping list had expanded as they went, and they were a half hour late.

Doug was sitting by the counter in a wheelchair, his robe wrapped around him, an angry look on his face. As soon as he saw her, he growled, "Where have you been? Are the boys all right?"

She forgave him his sharp words as she heard the worry in them. It wasn't that he didn't love his children. He just didn't know *how* to love them.

"They're fine, though they're really tired. We just had too much to do. We may have to come back next week. How are you?"

"Fine. Ready to go home."

"Do you want to ride up front or stretch out in the back?" she asked as he looked away from her.

"Front."

With such stimulating conversation, they were going to have a pleasant ride home, she decided. Then she caught herself. Not home—back to the ranch. She mustn't let herself start thinking of it as a permanent place for her. The man in front of her had made it plain that she'd be out the door as soon as the cast came off.

"Finished all your shopping?" Dr. Kelsey asked cheerfully as he strode up to them. "Ready to go?"

"Not really, but we were already late," she said, hoping he'd accept that as an apology.

"That doesn't matter. Doug has been down here only a few minutes. If you'd been on time, he wouldn't have been ready."

The doctor caught the frosty glare she sent Doug's way. "Oops. Was he giving you a hard time? Doug, shame on you."

"I'm ready to go home, so people will stop telling me how to behave," the rancher muttered, looking out the door where Leslie's car waited.

"You were right about this guy. He's been a grouch all day. But I guess we'll forgive him." The doctor leaned closer to Leslie to add quietly, "I've given him some more pain pills. Be sure he takes a couple of them when he gets home, and don't let him try to do too much too soon."

A quick glance showed her the pain lines around Doug's eyes, and she, too, forgave him his grouchiness. "I'll try. Thanks, Doctor. We'll be on our way."

"I'll get the guys to help you out."

"We don't need them," Doug snapped, flashing a look at the doctor, a look that Leslie couldn't read.

A half smile from the doctor told her he understood the silent message. He said, "I'll help you outside, then, but I think I'm going against my union rules." Before Doug could protest, Dr. Kelsey pushed the wheelchair out the door.

Leslie followed them. When she reached the car, she opened the driver's side to tell the boys to crawl into the back seat. If they were lucky, the boys would fall asleep on the pillows.

But the boys wanted to tell their dad all about the shopping trip. Leslie suggested they save their stories for after dinner because their dad was really tired. The doctor nodded in approval at Leslie's suggestion as he helped Doug fix his seat belt.

"I'm not an invalid, Jim," Doug protested.

"Nope. You're an ornery cuss, old son, but you're tired. Take it easy for a few days."

"Right." As the doctor started to close the door, he also muttered, "Thanks."

"No problem. Drive carefully, Leslie. We'll see you soon."

Leslie waved and then backed the car out of the parking lot. As she pulled onto the main road in the small town, she suggested the boys lie down. Before they could reach the city limits, both of them were asleep.

"You're good at that."

She was surprised that Doug was awake. His head had been back against the rest and his eyes had been closed. "What are you talking about?"

"The way you get the boys to do what you want." He closed his eyes again as if their conversation bored him.

"They were exhausted." When he said nothing about her explanation, she concentrated on her driving, trying to ignore how much smaller he made her car seem.

All week she'd avoided thinking of him, touching him, being near him. At least she'd tried. But it was hard to do when he was under her care. And then yesterday, when she'd put her arms around him to help him to the bathroom, she'd discovered trying to avoid him wasn't going to work.

It was too late.

When she'd arrived at the Bar-G Ranch, she'd been looking for a temporary solution to her aimlessness. A way to connect to someone. A bridge to her future.

But the attraction she felt for the man next to her, for his world, even for his children, was expanding at a terrifying rate. If the twins hadn't found them yesterday, after they fell onto the bed, she felt sure he would've kissed her. And the potential for that kiss had filled her with such hunger that she could scarcely concentrate.

"I've decided you're right."

She fought to remember what he could possibly be agreeing with. Surely he hadn't read her mind? No, his calm statement had nothing to do with kissing. She vaguely remembered something about the children going to sleep. Oh, yes, their following her suggestions. "Well, it's not surprising since they shopped for about six hours. That's—"

"That's not what I meant. I'm talking about Christmas."

Their leapfrog conversation wasn't easy to follow. Especially when her mind was on something much more enticing. "What about Christmas?"

"I haven't provided good Christmases for my children. Not like my mother did for me." He fell silent, but Leslie couldn't think of anything to say. She was too surprised.

"I'm going to change. And I want to say thank-you. You've shown me my duty."

She glanced at his determined face and then looked back at the road. "Doug, I'm glad you want to make Christmas special for your children, but—but why do you look so grim?"

"I'm not—" he began, his voice raised in frustration, when Leslie's finger to her lips reminded him of his sleeping children. "I'm not grim," he whispered. "You and Jim must be conspiring against me."

"Why?"

"Because he told me I should be happier about everything."

"Don't you like Christmas?"

Staring straight ahead, his lips pressed firmly together, he muttered, "I don't have anything against it."

After a moment of stunned silence, Leslie murmured, "That's not exactly an enthusiastic endorsement."

His eyes burned as he glared at her, and Leslie felt as if she'd just knocked over a bumblebee nest.

"The last few Christmases haven't... It's been difficult," he finished lamely, looking out the window.

They were on the open road, out of the city and any possible traffic, and Leslie let her glance slide to the man beside her. His rigid posture concerned her, and she reached out to touch his arm. Even through his jacket she felt the electric jolt his touch seemed to have on her.

He jumped and turned to stare at her again.

"I'm sorry," she said softly, withdrawing her hand. "I didn't mean to upset you."

Doug took a deep breath. The woman seemed to have no idea that his being this close to her put a huge strain on him. If he had his way, they'd pull over to the side of the road right now and—

He looked over the seat at his sleeping sons. So much for his resolution to be a good father. Making out with a woman while your children slept beside you wouldn't qualify you for Father of the Year. But the hunger growing inside him for Leslie was hard to handle.

Maybe it was all the lying around he'd been doing. Tomorrow he'd get back in the saddle, no matter what Jim said. He had to distract himself, or he'd be a victim of his hormones one more time.

Chapter Eight

Even after she dressed, Leslie rubbed the sleep from her eyes. She wasn't accustomed yet to getting up at the ungodly hour of five-thirty.

But in less than a half hour the cowboys would be entering the bunkhouse kitchen for their breakfast. She started for the stairs, but the sound of someone stirring in Doug's bedroom halted her rush.

She tapped lightly on the door.

It swung open abruptly. "Yeah?" Doug asked, frowning at her.

"Are you all right? I'm going to the bunkhouse. Do you need something before I go?" He'd taken the pain pills without complaint yesterday afternoon and gone to sleep at about eight last night.

"No. I'm going with you."

His squared jaw told her he was expecting an argument.

He was right, though she'd prefer to leave him alone, to keep her distance. *Yeah, right, Leslie,* a little voice mocked her.

"Dr. Kelsey said for you to take it easy for a few days," she reminded him.

"My men have been working long hours, trying to make up for my absence. It's time I'm back in the saddle."

"But you can't get jeans over your cast and you'll freeze to death in those shorts." Even though the shorts he wore gave her a clear view of his muscular thighs—a view she thoroughly appreciated.

"I can put ski pants over my leg. With all those zippers, it's easy. But I might need a little help," he added, glaring at her as if it were her fault.

His walking cast only came to below his knee, so getting on the ski pants wouldn't be difficult. But mounting a horse and riding even half a day would be a strain. She could tell by the square set of his jaw, however, that arguing would be wasted breath.

"Okay." She walked over to the bed where the ski pants were waiting. Unzipping both leg zippers, she handed the pants to him. Once he'd wrapped them around his long legs, she knelt and zipped up his good leg. Then she moved to his broken leg and started the zipper at the waist. He lifted up his arm to give her more room, and the fantasy of being in his embrace was almost too real.

Breathing became a struggle as his arm held her close to him. She couldn't keep from looking up at his face, to see if he, too, was experiencing difficulty.

It was as if he were waiting for her. Their gazes met and held, the naked hunger in his a reflection of her own feelings. His mouth lowered to hers as his arm pulled her up and against him. The kiss she'd fantasized about for so long was more powerful than she'd imagined it could be. She lost herself in his touch, her hands traveling up his T-shirt-covered chest, seeking his heat. When his tongue sought hers, she put up no resistance. How could she when his touch made her feel she'd come home?

This time when they fell on the bed, it wasn't an accident but the culmination of desire. Leslie wrapped her arms around his strong body, her hands sliding beneath his T-shirt to knead and massage his back, to urge him closer. His lips left hers to explore the soft skin of her neck and she felt shivers down to her toes. His touch was electrifying.

His lips returned to hers and she was lost to reality, feeling such a belonging, a welcoming sensation that filled her both with joy and excitement such as she'd never experienced. What was happening was so right, she had no thought of putting an end to it.

Doug leaned back just enough to slide his warm hand up her sweater to caress one breast even as he kissed her, and Leslie groaned. She hadn't realized a man's touch could feel so good, so overpowering. Her tension, her need increased as he stroked her, kissed her, and she bucked beneath him for more.

He rolled off her and Leslie was shocked by the immediate depression that filled her. But it was quickly relieved when he whisked her sweater off and pulled her back to him. His lips caressed her shoulder, nudging her bra strap down inch by excruciating inch.

She tugged at his T-shirt, wanting equal privilege, aching to caress his hot skin with her lips, to feel the powerful muscles, to touch him everywhere. She scarcely noticed her breasts were freed until his lips found one. The exquisite ache that filled her brought a crooning to her lips, a cry of need that softly filled the room.

His mouth returned to hers, as if in answer to her cry, and his hands continued to work their magic on her body. She was on the edge of paradise when he abruptly rolled away, lying on the bed with his back to her.

"Doug?" she whispered, her voice filled with the ache of loss. What had happened?

He rolled back over but kept a careful distance between them. "My apologies, Leslie. You'd be wise to keep your distance from now on."

His words brought shame to what had been a glorious experience. She refastened her bra and quickly sought her sweater. When her clothes were back in place, she faced him. "You make it sound like this was my fault."

"No, of course not," he said in a carefully controlled voice, his gaze fastened to the ceiling. "We both got carried away. In fact, it's my fault. I should have been prepared for this ever since you answered the ad."

"What are you talking about?" she asked, confused.

He didn't look at her. "Please. Let's not pretend. I've been down this road before. Just take care of the boys and the house. I'll handle my... my things."

Anger, both at his dismissive words and at her own desires, still raging within her, brought her to her feet. "I can assure you, Mr. Graybow, I won't tempt you again!"

She slammed the door behind her as she exited the room and then remembered the boys, sleeping only a few feet away. With a shrug of her shoulders, she headed out on to the bunkhouse.

Doug didn't move for at least five minutes. It took that long to bring his raging body back under control. He'd thought he'd had the hots for Bettina, but that attraction had been a young man's adventure into sex. What he'd just experienced had been a man's desire for a woman, a powerful desire that almost made him forget everything.

That's what he'd almost done. He'd almost forgotten her intention to marry him. He'd almost forgotten what a disaster marriage was for him. He'd almost forgotten to stay in control.

AFTER A BRIEF, tense encounter with Doug over breakfast, Leslie decided she deserved a break. She trudged up the slight hill, holding her coat close against her to keep out the wind. When she reached the house, it was almost seven. The boys were sitting on the top stair, waiting for her. So much for a break.

"Hi, Leslie. We woke up and everybody was gone. Where's Daddy?"

"He decided to work today. Come on down and we'll fix breakfast."

They didn't hesitate. Like the hungry males she'd just fed, these two had a roaring appetite every morning. In spite of the work, there was something satisfying about cooking for them.

As they ate, she couldn't help but wonder what it would be like to have a family of her own. To sit across the table from her own children and husband, and share plans for the morning or remembrances of the day. Leslie knew this was what she wanted. And she'd find it—eventually. But she'd best remember Justin and Gareth were Doug's family, and he was her employer.

To clear her mind, she cleaned up the dishes and afterward they spread out all their purchases for the Christmas tree on the living room floor. The boys argued over where to put the tree, finally deciding on the front window. Then Leslie led them to the kitchen to make Christmas cookies.

Hours later, just as they were clearing a space in all their preparations to have sandwiches and soup for lunch, there was a knock at the front door. Thinking Doug might have come back early, she rushed out to the hallway in spite of herself.

"Is it Daddy?" Gareth asked, fast on her heels.

"I don't know. It might be."

"Why would he knock?" Justin asked, puzzled.

That question slowed Leslie. "I don't know."

She swung the door open to find a stranger standing there. He was dressed like a cowboy, in boots, jeans, a heavy jacket and a Stetson.

"Morning, ma'am. Is Mr. Graybow here?"

It occurred to Leslie that she was there alone with two small boys and no protection. But she wasn't suspicious by nature, so she dismissed that momentary concern. "No, he's not in the house. Come in out of the cold."

"Thank you," he said, and stepped into the hallway. "Can I help you?"

"Well, I heard in town Mr. Graybow was lookin' for some help and I'm lookin' for a job. Dr. Kelsey thought maybe he'd take me on. The doc said he'd give me a recommendation."

"I'm sure he'd like to talk to you. He should be back in an hour or two. Can you wait?"

"Sure. I'll just sit in my pickup until—" The dark stranger turned to go back out into the cold.

"No, don't do that." If Dr. Kelsey was willing to vouch for him, the man couldn't be a threat. "It's too cold to sit outside. Come in and I'll fix you a cup of coffee. Have you had lunch?"

"No, ma'am, but I don't expect you to—"

"It's no trouble."

In the warmth of the kitchen the man relaxed and settled at the table with a cup of coffee as Leslie prepared the sandwiches.

"I appreciate your hospitality, ma'am. My name's Steven Holcomb."

"You're welcome. I'm Leslie, and these two are Gareth and Justin."

"We're twins," Gareth said importantly.

"I can see that."

Soon the boys were entertaining their guest and lunch was a cozy affair. They were all laughing at Justin's attempt to decorate one of the Christmas cookies afterward when the kitchen door was shoved open.

Looking half-frozen and exhausted, Doug stood staring at them, a ferocious frown on his face. Before anyone could speak, he glared at Leslie and demanded, "Who's that?" gesturing toward the cowboy sitting in his place at the table.

Before Leslie could answer, the twins erupted from their chairs and ran to hug his legs, exclaiming at his early return.

Steve, as Leslie and the boys had begun to call him, stood, taking his Stetson in his hand, as if ready to bolt the house at a moment's notice.

Leslie had to admit there wasn't much sign of hospitality in Doug's voice. She hadn't expected any warmth for herself, but Steve was a guest. She stepped forward. "Doug, this is Steven Holcomb. He heard from Dr. Kelsey that you needed another hand and came to talk to you." When Doug didn't respond, she added, "I asked him to wait."

"Sorry if I'm intruding, Mr. Graybow. Your wife said I could wait here instead of in my truck, but—"

Leslie, after a startled look at Steve, began to correct his mistake, but Doug spoke before she could.

"Of course. And I do need some help. Could you wait in the living room for a minute?"

Even the twins were silent as Steve left the room, putting his hat back on his head before tipping it at Leslie and thanking her for her hospitality.

She smiled in return and then discovered Doug glaring at her again.

As soon as the four of them were alone, she said, "I didn't tell him I was your wife, Doug. He must have just assumed—"

"If you were Daddy's wife, would you be our mommy?" Gareth asked.

"Yes, sweetie, but—"

"Boys, go watch television." His tone of voice invited no resistance and the two scampered out the kitchen and up the stairs.

"It's not their fault, Doug—"

"No, it's your fault," he roared at Leslie, his temper exploding. "How could you be crazy enough to invite a stranger into the house with just you and the boys here?"

Leslie stared at him in surprise. She'd thought he was angry about Steve's assumption; instead he'd been worried about them? "But, Doug, it's cold outside."

"I know that! I'm half damn frozen! But he could've been a rapist, a murderer—who knows what, Leslie! You can't just—"

"I wouldn't have asked him in if I'd thought he'd be a danger to the kids. He's very nice and Dr. Kelsey recommended him. And you do need another hand." She stood her ground, a little tired of his anger. She hadn't done anything wrong. In fact, she'd been trying to help.

"I know, I know." He shrugged, the fight suddenly going out of his voice, replaced by exhaustion.

"Sit down and let me pour you a cup of coffee," Leslie insisted. As soon as he'd complied with her suggestion, she began heating up some soup left over from lunch.

"What's all this?" he asked, waving to the cookie-making mess that covered more than half the table.

"The boys and I have been making Christmas cookies. Most of them are baked, but now we have to decorate them."

He stared at the cookies shaped like Christmas trees, bells, candy canes and gifts. Then he picked up a different shape. "Boots?"

"Well, I found that cookie cutter and I thought it would be cute for Christmas since the boys live on a ranch."

"My mother used it when she made sugar cookies." He seemed lost in thought as he held the still-warm cookie.

"You can eat that one, if you want, but don't touch one of the decorated ones until the boys show them to you." Each of the twins had labored over their first decorations. Leslie knew from experience that the thrill would wear off before the afternoon was over, but the first ones were special.

While Doug munched on the cookie, Leslie wondered what should be done about Steve. She didn't know about his cowboy skills, but he was a nice man. If he started work on the ranch, it would take some of the pressure off Doug. Just as she was going to ask Doug to interview him, the front door opened and Moss called out a greeting.

Leslie heard his surprise as he came upon Steve.

"Hello. Sorry, I didn't know the boss had company."

Doug got up slowly and limped out to the hallway, where he introduced the two men. When he invited them back into the kitchen, Leslie was pleased and poured two more cups of coffee.

"How'd you know I wanted coffee, Les?" Moss teased, warming his hands on the hot cup.

"I think it was the frost on the window, Moss. Was it cold out today?"

"Not if we was polar bears."

"I'll go upstairs and keep the boys busy while you talk," Leslie said after smiling at Moss's joke. Doug nodded and watched her until she left the room.

Once the door had closed behind her, the man across from him smiled and said, "You're a lucky man. Your wife is not only beautiful, she's a great mother and cook."

Doug glowered at him. The man's words awoke an unexpected envy in him. He'd thought, when he married Bettina, that he'd come in from a hard day's work to find his wife waiting for him, a warm kitchen, good food, a child waiting to hug his daddy. It hadn't happened.

Until now. With Leslie. Who wasn't even his wife.

"Yep, the boss is a lucky man," Moss agreed. Doug turned to look at him and discovered Moss had one eyebrow raised in question. He realized Moss would play along with the charade if he wanted him to. But he couldn't.

"She's my housekeeper," Doug said gruffly. The light that came into the cowboy's eyes with that piece of information disturbed him, but Moss turned the questions to the man's past experience. Soon the three of them were discussing ranching techniques and common acquaintances.

Within a quarter hour, Doug knew he'd be crazy not to offer Steve a job. And he wasn't crazy. But the man's response to Leslie bothered him.

"Uh, by the way, Leslie's only temporary." He hadn't intended his words to sound so abrupt, but they did.

"Oh?"

"I just didn't want you to get used to her cooking. As soon as we're fully staffed again and I get this cast off my leg, Leslie will be returning to Kansas City."

"That's too bad," Steve said.

"Yeah" was Moss's heartfelt agreement. "That lady makes the best apple pie I've ever tasted."

"She doesn't want to stay?" Steve asked.

"Her home is Kansas City. She's just helping out as a favor," Doug replied, not answering his question but hoping to bring an end to the discussion.

Steve nodded, and Doug was relieved.

"We'd like to have you join us, Steve. I'm satisfied with your experience. Do you have any questions?"

The offer of a job grabbed Steve's attention and he accepted it. Just as Doug relaxed, however, he spoke again. "I do have one question. Are there any rules against dating the temporary housekeeper?"

Doug glared at the cowboy. "I don't think it'd be a good idea." He refused to explain for whom.

LESLIE WENT UP the stairs with her fingers crossed. She hoped Doug wouldn't let his anger about her actions keep him from hiring the new man. His work today had obviously exhausted him. With Steve in the saddle, perhaps she could keep Doug at the house for a few days, until he was stronger.

Not that it was her business, she reminded herself. All day she'd lectured herself about her situation. She was here to keep house, to take care of the boys. Certainly she was not going to ever touch Doug Graybow again . . . or invite his touch.

No, she was just hoping for what would be best for everyone.

The boys had turned the television to a cartoon station and sat with their eyes glued to the screen. But as soon as she sat down on a nearby chair, they ran to her.

"Leslie, we know what we want Santa to bring us!" Justin exclaimed.

Leslie and the twins had talked about writing letters to Santa while they baked. She'd told them to start thinking about what they would request. "Good. Then you'll be ready to write your letters to Santa first thing Monday morning."

"We want to write them now!" Gareth exclaimed.

"What about decorating the Christmas cookies? We have to finish them, don't we?"

The boys pleaded to start the letters now. Since she didn't know how long the interview downstairs would take, she changed her mind. "Find some paper and a pencil and you can start your letters."

As soon as the necessary items were found, each boy stretched out on his stomach and began copying Leslie's carefully printed letters for "Dear Santa."

"Now, you have to tell me what you want Santa to bring you and I'll print it out for you to copy," she said, waiting patiently.

"We want you to be our mommy!" Justin exclaimed. "That's what we're going to ask Santa for."

Leslie stared at the two children, shocked. Finally she cleared her throat. "That's very sweet of you, boys, but you can't ask Santa for a person."

"Don't you want to be our mommy?" Gareth asked, crawling over to kneel beside her and stroke her hair as he watched her carefully.

"I'd love it, sweetheart, but it's not possible." She suddenly realized that she was telling the truth. The twins weren't perfect, of course, but she was coming to love them.

"Yes, it is," Justin explained. "You said if you married Daddy, you'd be our mommy."

Almost groaning aloud, Leslie hastily tried to think of a logical explanation. After what had happened this morning, Doug would probably accuse her of putting the boys up to this idea. "But your daddy doesn't want to marry me, Justin." She knew that for sure after this morning's rejection. "That's not something you should ask Santa Claus for. Why don't you ask him for—for a puppy? That's what you should ask for," she repeated, suddenly enthusiastic. "A puppy you could train to protect you."

A flicker of excitement filled both boys' faces, but then they dismissed her idea.

"That'd be nice, but we'd rather have you," Justin explained.

Leslie smoothed back the mop of hair that fell over his forehead, just like his father's, and smiled. "That's really nice, but like I said, you can't ask Santa for people."

"But, Leslie—" Justin protested.

"No, Justin. Just take my word for it. I'm going down to see if your father is finished with the kitchen." She escaped at once, anxious to be alone. Those two towheaded imps were getting harder and harder to resist. Blinking her eyes to dismiss any stray tears, she reminded herself, "I'll be leaving in three weeks. I'll be leaving in three weeks. I'll be leaving—" She broke off with a sob.

"DO YOU THINK Leslie doesn't want to be our mother?" Gareth asked, staring at the door.

Justin frowned, staring in the same direction, as he considered his answer. "No. She loves us. Agnes didn't ever give us hugs and kisses like Leslie does."

"Then why did she say no?"

Justin didn't have an answer to that question and it worried him. "Maybe we haven't been good enough."

"I don't think we'd better try being good again. The last time we did, Daddy said we caused lots of 'havoc,' whatever that is."

"But Leslie hugged us anyway. She said we had good 'tentions." Justin thought a little longer. "Maybe we should ask Daddy to help us with our letters. I think it's the man who's supposed to ask the lady."

"Hey, you're right, 'cause the man always gives the lady a present. Do you think we embarrassed Leslie?"

"No. Her face wasn't red like it was when she and Daddy were on the bed. But I think we need Daddy to help us. Daddy and Santa Claus."

WHISPERS PENETRATED Doug's sleep and he reluctantly stirred awake. After hiring Steve, he'd decided to rest for a while, which allowed him to avoid Leslie. He wasn't finding it as easy as he'd hoped to ignore what had happened this morning. Or to control his body. It had taken him a long time to go to sleep.

"Do you think he's awake yet?" one of his twins whispered.

"He hasn't opened his eyes. Maybe we should—"

Doug was afraid of what tactics they might consider if he didn't let them know he was awake. Opening his eyes, he discovered one on each side of him, their noses only inches from his.

"You're awake," Gareth declared in satisfaction.

"I didn't have much choice with the two of you whispering in my ears," he complained, but he smiled to let them know he wasn't really upset.

"It's almost dinnertime," Justin told him. "Leslie said she'd have to wake you up soon so you could go to sleep tonight." He frowned. "Isn't that silly, Daddy? To wake you up so you can sleep?"

"It sounds a little confusing, but I know what Leslie meant." Doug was feeling much better than he had when he'd first come in from the cold. In fact, he was feeling great, he realized, as he stretched under the cover.

"We need to talk to you, Daddy." Gareth seemed to want to get right down to whatever he had on his mind.

Doug struggled to sit up and the boys pushed pillows behind him. "Okay."

"We need to talk about Christmas. We don't got no money."

"Any money," Doug corrected.

"No," Justin agreed. "We don't."

"What do you need money for?"

"How will we buy presents? Leslie says Christmas is when you give presents to people you love," Justin explained.

"Ah. And did Leslie say you should go buy something for her, maybe?" He still couldn't help being a little suspicious of her.

"Oh, no. She said we could make presents. We're decorating cookies for Moss and the other cowboys. She said they'd love something to eat," Gareth said.

"She's right about that."

"And we decorated them ourselves." Justin looked so proud of himself. "I put silver balls on a Christmas tree 'specially for Moss."

"He'll like that, son."

"The money, Justin," Gareth prodded.

"But Leslie helped us, Daddy, and we don't want to give her something she helped with," Justin said in response to his brother's reminder.

"That's thoughtful of you. I suppose we could go shopping for a present for Leslie, and I could pay for it. Maybe if you polished my boots for me in return?"

The boys eagerly nodded in agreement, but Gareth added, "And maybe we could do something else so we could buy a present for you too?"

"I believe that could be arranged." Doug was pleased by their generosity. "I could give some money to Leslie—that you earned, of course—" he hurriedly inserted, "and Leslie could help you shop for me."

"Good," Justin said, "so it can be a surprise. Leslie says the best thing about Christmas is being surprised by people who love you."

Doug couldn't hold back memories of the times in the past when his parents had made Christmas special for him. "I believe Leslie's right about that."

"Yeah," Gareth agreed, nodding his head.

Doug waited to see what else his children wanted to talk about. Before Leslie's arrival, he couldn't remember time spent like this, the three of them together. He'd always been in a hurry, or had turned over the child-rearing responsibility to Agnes.

Justin ran a hesitant finger over a fold in the sheet, his gaze following the movement with great concentration. Gareth watched with equal fascination.

"Is there something else you wanted to ask, boys?" Doug asked curiously.

"Well..." Justin began, drawing out the one word.

"Boys?" Leslie called up the stairs softly.

The two jumped as if they'd been caught in a terrible sin.

"What's the matter?"

"Leslie told us not to bother you," Gareth whispered as he began to scramble off the bed, his brother quickly following.

"They're with me, Leslie," Doug called. The boys stood by the bed as they all listened to her footsteps.

She opened the door to discover the three of them watching for her. "They didn't wake you up, did they?" she asked stiffly. He noticed she didn't cross the threshold to his room.

"I was waking up and feeling a little lonely. They agreed to keep me company."

"That was kind of them." Her brief smile was directed at his sons. "Since you're awake, would you like dinner up here?"

"No, I think I'll come to the table. I've eaten in bed enough lately to last me a lifetime." He'd also eaten alone too much lately. A cozy meal in the kitchen with Leslie and the boys sounded good, even if it did involve a strain on his self-control.

"All right. Dinner in five minutes. Boys, go wash your hands before you come down to set the table." She closed the door and was gone before anyone answered.

"What did you want to ask me?" Doug asked, when he finally drew his attention back to his children.

"We can't ask now, Daddy. We have to set the table," Gareth said, starting for the door.

"You don't mind helping Leslie?" Doug asked.

"No. It helps us learn," Justin explained. On his way out the door, he added, "We'll ask our question later, but not in front of Leslie, okay?"

"Okay." The boys must be trying to decide what kind of present to buy her. He supposed he'd need to buy her something, too. A bottle of perfume or something.

He slid from the bed and headed to his own bathroom, trying to ignore the sudden memory of the light floral fragrance that always filled the room when Leslie entered.

"DADDY, DID YOU HIRE Steve?" Gareth asked just before he took a big bite of chicken casserole.

Doug let his gaze flash to Leslie's face, seeing the interest there in his answer. Why did she care? Had she been attracted to the man? Jealousy flared full-size in his stomach.

"Yes, I hired him."

"He liked our cookies," Justin said, filling an awkward silence.

"Me, too. Are we having them for dessert?"

"No," both boys exclaimed. "Those are for Christmas presents."

"Well, I hope I'm going to be included on the present list, because they looked delicious," Doug assured his sons. Their beaming smiles were his reward.

"I made chocolate cake for dessert." Leslie rose abruptly to clear the table.

"My favorite." He spoke without looking at her. It amazed him that she'd had time, knowing she'd been busy with the Christmas cookies and the house and kids.

"Good. I'd like to ask a favor." Leslie had turned back to the table from the sink and wasn't looking at him, either.

"Sure. I probably owe you at least half a dozen for all you've done." He wondered what she had in mind.

"Would you keep an eye on the twins while I run into town? I shouldn't be gone more than a couple of hours."

"But it's almost dark now," he protested automatically, his gaze going to the window over the kitchen sink.

"I know, but the weather's clear, and I'll be back before nine."

In spite of his resistance to the idea, he agreed. He even held back the questions that flooded his mind. Was she going into town to party? To have a drink with the cowboys? To meet someone he didn't know? He had no right to ask those questions, particularly after his words this morning.

"Thanks," she said, wiping her hands on a tea towel. "I'll just go get my coat and purse. Boys, be good for your daddy tonight. I'll be back in time to tuck you in."

"You are coming back, aren't you, Leslie?" Justin asked.

Leslie seemed to take Justin's concern seriously. "Of course I am. I wouldn't leave without saying goodbye, and I'm leaving all my belongings upstairs. Okay?"

"Okay." Justin seemed satisfied with her explanation.

She kissed his cheek and Gareth's before going out the door.

A stillness settled over the house, as if its life spark had died away. Doug shook himself from such a ridiculous thought. It was the quietness that had made him think such a thing.

"Well, boys, how shall we spend the evening?" he asked with false heartiness, trying to dispel the sudden loneliness.

"I think we'd better ask you our question," Gareth said, looking at his brother.

"Yeah, 'cause usually Leslie's here," Justin added.

"Okay, what question?" Doug asked, waiting. In his enjoyment of the evening meal, he'd forgotten their interrupted conversation.

"We wanted to ask you about Santa Claus," Justin explained.

Doug cocked one eyebrow and looked at his children. Were they going to ask him if Santa was real? What was he supposed to answer? He couldn't remember when his parents had told him the man in the red suit was a fantasy.

"We wanted to know if he's really good," Gareth said.

"Good? You mean, is he nice?"

"No, we mean will he bring us what we ask for?" Justin asked. He got down from his chair and came around the table to lean against Doug's arm. "Will he?"

The caution that parents learn early reared its head. "Well," Doug said, clearing away a sudden huskiness,

"I'm sure he'd try his best. Sometimes it's not possible."

Gareth came to his other side. "Maybe if you helped him? He could do it then, couldn't he?"

"I don't know, son. You'd better tell me what you're wanting him to bring." He was getting an ominous feeling that their request wasn't going to be easy.

Two pairs of big brown eyes were trained on his face as his children pressed against him. Finally Justin said, "We want Leslie as our mama for Christmas."

Chapter Nine

Doug finally shut his gaping mouth and cleared his throat. He was tempted to ask his children to repeat their request, but he really didn't want to hear it again. "I'm afraid that's not possible."

"Why not?" Gareth demanded. "She doesn't have any kids of her own. And she loves us."

Justin pushed his way into his father's lap and leaned his head back to look up at him. "We don't remember our real mama, and Leslie makes everything so nice."

Doug cleared his throat again. "Yes, yes, she does make everything nice, but—but Santa can't bring people."

"That's what Leslie said," Gareth muttered.

"You told Leslie?"

"Yeah, and she said we should ask for a dog instead. If it was okay with you," Gareth hurriedly added.

Doug told himself he was relieved that Leslie hadn't gone along with the boys' idea. Of course he was. But why hadn't she? Was she not interested in marrying him? And if she wasn't, why had she come here?

Maybe she changed her mind after this morning. That thought didn't do much for his ego. But then, not many of his encounters with Leslie had.

"A dog is great. That's a good idea. I should have gotten one sooner, but Agnes didn't like dogs in the house and I just put it off. Great! We'll get a dog. How about a Labrador? That would be—"

"Daddy," Justin said, tugging his arm impatiently.

"What, son?"

"We don't need Santa."

"What do you mean, Justin?"

"Santa can bring us a dog. We'd like that, but if he can't bring us Leslie, we know how we can do it."

He didn't like the sound of Justin's words. "How?"

"You just marry her. Then she'd be our mama forever." When his father didn't answer, Justin asked anxiously, "Wouldn't she?"

Swinging Justin from his knee, Doug struggled upright to take his cup across the room to the coffeepot. With his back to those bright eyes, he muttered, "Uh, yes, if we got married, but that's not a very good idea."

"Why not?" Gareth had crossed the room to stand beside him.

"Because marriage is something special that shouldn't happen unless—unless two people really love each other."

"Like you and Mama?" Justin asked, joining his brother to block Doug's path across the kitchen floor.

Damn! What should he say now? No, your mama and I got married because she was pregnant? Or should he lie to them, sacrificing his own standards for his sons' happiness?

"Uh, I need to sit down, boys. My leg is hurting."

Their sudden care brought a smile to Doug's face in spite of his dilemma. More hindrance than help, they each took a hand and led him back to his chair.

"Tell us, Daddy," Gareth demanded as he stood by his father's chair.

"Tell you what, Gareth?"

"About our real mama and why Leslie can't be our mama."

"Well, when two people marry, it's because they, uh, love each other. A lot."

"We love Leslie a lot. Lots and lots," Justin assured him, his little face serious.

"And she loves us," Gareth repeated.

"Yes, but you wouldn't be the ones marrying Leslie. Well, not exactly. I'd be the husband." He dismissed the fleeting warmth that thought brought.

"And you don't love Leslie?" Justin asked, disbelief in his voice. "She took care of you when you couldn't walk. And she made you a chocolate cake."

"Those things would make her a really good mama, or a housekeeper, but they don't qualify her to be a wife."

"What does a wife have to do?" Gareth asked.

He'd certainly painted himself into a corner now. How could he explain such a complex relationship to five-year-olds? "Uh, a wife has to love her husband and—and be willing to have more babies," he finished in a rush. That should take care of it. He wouldn't need to explain the attraction that a husband should feel, that thrumming of tension whenever she was in a room, that urge to touch her for no reason at all.

He knew he'd made a mistake when the boys' eyes rounded in silent awe. "What?" he asked worriedly.

"You mean if you married Leslie, we could have babies instead of puppies?" Justin asked. Gareth didn't bother with clarification. He began to dance around the kitchen whooping at the top of his voice.

"Would they be more twins?" Justin asked, beaming.

That question got Gareth's attention. "Yeah, would they be like us, only littler?"

"We could teach 'em everything," Justin said without waiting for an answer to his question, staring into the distance as if he could see those new siblings. "Leslie would want our help. Daddy, how many babies could we have? When Johnny Wester's dog had puppies, there were six of them!"

"No! Wait! I didn't mean— We can't— You're way off track," Doug protested, panic filling him.

"What do you mean? We can't have six babies? How many could we have? Four?" Justin guessed.

"No. None. We can't have any more babies."

"Why?" Gareth demanded, anger in his voice.

"Leslie likes babies, Daddy," Justin explained. "She told us she wanted to have babies. Remember, Gareth?"

"Yeah. Don't you want more babies, Daddy?" Gareth asked, somewhat appeased by his brother's words but intent all the same on winning their argument.

Doug drew a deep breath and opened his arms to his children. Talk about opening a can of worms! As his sons snuggled against him, he said, "Boys, if I could have more babies like you two, I would. But—but that's not all Leslie would have to do, you know. There's lots more."

"Like what?" Gareth demanded, unwilling to let go of their plans.

"Um, she couldn't have her own room. She'd have to share mine, and she wouldn't like that. And—" he thought frantically before adding "—she wouldn't get paid to do all this work. She'd have to do it for free."

"How come?"

"'Cause that's what wives do."

"What else?" Justin asked.

He was getting desperate. He had to come up with something the boys would understand. Something that would make Leslie becoming his wife unbearable . . . for Leslie. What did they hate most? A sudden inspiration filled him. "She'd have to dress up every Sunday and go to church."

"Oh, no," Gareth whispered. "Are you sure? Would she have to sit real still?"

"She couldn't move," Doug embellished, eager to dissuade them. "And she'd have to wear a skirt and nylons and lots of girl things. Leslie doesn't have a skirt."

"I bet she does," Justin said faintly, as if his hope was already fading.

"I sure haven't seen her wearing one," Doug pointed out, but he felt mean. He was sure Leslie owned skirts, but she hadn't worn any since her arrival. Perhaps his statement wasn't quite accurate, but it worked for him.

"She'd look pretty in a skirt, wouldn't she?" Justin asked wistfully, a sadness on his face that made Doug's gut wrench.

"Yeah, son, she'd look terrific." In fact, he'd fantasized a time or two about Leslie in a skirt. Or out of one.

Gareth reclaimed his straying attention. "Tomorrow's Sunday, isn't it?" At Doug's nod, he said, "Do we have to go to church without Leslie?"

"I think we should."

"But what will you wear, Daddy? Your leg is real fat with that cast thing."

"Uh, I don't know," Doug responded to Gareth's question. "We'll try to figure out something in the morning. Now, how about we do the dishes for Leslie and then go upstairs to watch television. I think there's another Christmas special on tonight."

The boys agreed, but they didn't show the enthusiasm they'd felt earlier. Maybe he really was Scrooge, stealing their Christmas. Hell, he wasn't too happy about the holidays himself.

LESLIE COULD HEAR the television as she entered the house. Since the kitchen was dark, she assumed the three Graybows would be watching a program together in Doug's bedroom.

When she reached the top of the stairs, she knocked on the open door. "Hi. I'm back."

"Leslie!" Justin exclaimed and slid off the bed to hurry to her side. His arms wrapped around her as if he had been afraid she wouldn't return.

"Hi, sweetheart. Were you good while I was gone?"

"They were both terrific," Doug answered in place of his son. He still felt guilty about the boys' disappointment.

"What did you buy?" Gareth asked, noticing the packages she held in one hand.

"Gareth, you shouldn't ask such a personal question," Doug reprimanded.

"It's all right. I wasn't doing any Christmas shopping tonight, Gareth. I just wanted to find something to wear to church tomorrow."

A deathly stillness filled the room that surprised Leslie. Suddenly Gareth whooped and flopped back against his father.

"What—"

"Do you really want to go to church, Leslie?" Justin asked in a hushed voice. "You have to be real still."

She smiled. "Of course I do. I always go back home, and Moss said you usually go to Sunday school and church every Sunday. I thought you'd want me to take you in case your dad can't go."

"You always go to church? And you wear girl clothes?" Gareth asked, an intent look on his face.

"Girl clothes?" Leslie asked, frowning.

"You know, a skirt and—and things. You remember, Daddy, like you told us," Gareth said, jabbing his elbow into his father's stomach.

Leslie wondered if Doug wasn't feeling well. He looked a little green behind the gills. Or maybe Gareth had hit a sensitive spot. "Doug, are you all right?"

"Fine. I'm fine. And that's very thoughtful of you to offer, but I think the boys—all of us—should stay home in the morning."

"Of course, if you don't want the boys to go to church, they can stay here with you. But I'd like to go. I'll fix breakfast beforehand, and it won't take long to cook dinner when I get back. That will be all right, won't it?"

Doug's face looked as if he were struggling to find an appropriate answer. She frowned. What could be so difficult about letting her go to church?

"Sure. That will be fine."

"I want to go if Leslie is going," Justin said, pressing more closely against her.

"Me, too!" Gareth exclaimed. "I bet she can be still a long time. And wear girl clothes."

"Were you afraid I'd want to wear jeans?" Leslie asked the little boy.

"We haven't seen you in a skirt. But Daddy said you'd look real pretty in one," Gareth explained.

Leslie's cheeks flamed as her gaze ricocheted off Doug's startled look. "That's—that's very nice of your father. I should have brought a skirt, but I packed in a hurry, kind of impulsively," she said in a rush before she realized she was rambling. "I'd be glad for you to go to church with me if your father doesn't mind." She hoped the change of subject would cool off her cheeks.

"Can we, Daddy?" the boys pleaded.

Again Doug appeared frustrated. She wondered what was going through his mind. "We'll all go," he replied gruffly.

As grouchy as he sounded, Leslie decided it was time for the boys to go to bed. The boys, on the other hand, seemed ridiculously excited. It would be hard to settle them down to sleep.

"It's time for your bath, boys. I'll go run your water."

"Yes, Leslie," they chorused like little angels, and ran from the room.

"Is everything all right? Are you tired?" she asked quietly as Doug stared at the television.

"Fine. I'm fine."

"Did the boys behave?"

"Yes. But they told me what they want Santa to bring them." He turned to glare at her.

"Do you disapprove? I'm sorry. I didn't think you'd mind," she said, stiffening at his obvious disapproval. A dog had been the best idea she'd been able to come up with after such a shock.

"Mind? Not mind? What— Oh. You're talking about the dog."

When she realized what he'd been talking about—the boys' original request—her cheeks flamed again. "I didn't put them up to that idea, Doug. It was just as big a surprise to me as it was to you."

"I know."

"I explained that it wasn't possible."

"I did, too."

"Good. Then we'll just concentrate on a dog. If that's okay with you."

"A dog is fine."

She stood there awkwardly, unable to think of anything else to say. "I—I'll go run the bathwater."

"Fine."

If he said "fine" one more time, she thought she'd scream. Obviously, everything was not fine, but she didn't know what to do about it.

As she turned to go, Doug spoke again.

"Leslie, about this morning..."

She didn't—couldn't—turn around. Instead, she stood as still as a statue, waiting for whatever he had to say.

"That can't happen again."

Irritation spun her around. "You mean I shouldn't try to seduce you anymore?" she demanded, outraged that he seemed to be putting the blame on her.

He sat up, leaning toward her, and said in a low voice, "I wasn't blaming you. It just—just happened. But I'm not going to marry again. You should know that by now."

"I don't believe I asked you!" she snapped, stunned by his words.

"Come on, Leslie. We both know—"

"Leslie? Are you coming?" Justin called.

"Just a minute," she returned before facing Doug again. "I don't know what you think you know, Douglas Graybow, but I can promise you seduction isn't on my résumé." She stormed from the room without waiting for a response.

LESLIE LED THE BOYS to their Sunday school class, holding a clean hand in each of hers. She was proud of their appearance—their shirts freshly ironed, their hair slicked back. They'd been willing participants in the morning's preparations.

Which was more than she could say for Doug. He'd been a grouch all morning. Even the breakfast she'd cooked hadn't pleased him. For some reason, he'd lost his appetite.

When she'd offered to split the seam on his pant leg in order to have it fit over the cast, he'd protested. His starched white shirt hadn't pleased him. And when he'd finally given in to her opening the seam on his dress pants, he'd wanted to supervise her work.

Now he was stomping along behind them, his irregular gait only emphasizing his unhappiness.

"This is our room, Leslie. Do you want to meet Mrs. Meggy, our teacher?" Justin asked.

"I'd love to." She ignored the growl from behind.

"Mrs. Meggy," Justin called, not turning loose of Leslie's hand.

Leslie watched as a pretty young blonde turned toward them.

"Justin, Gareth, I wasn't sure you'd be here since your dad broke his leg."

"Leslie brought us," Gareth explained. "And Daddy came, too," he added.

Leslie turned loose of the boys' hands and extended her right one to their teacher. "I'm Leslie Hibbets, the temporary housekeeper at the Bar-G Ranch."

"I'm delighted to meet you. My name is Meggy Anderson. My husband and I are near neighbors. I should've been over to meet you, but I haven't been feeling too well lately."

Though she gave Leslie the once-over, Leslie didn't mind. She would've done the same in the circumstances. The woman's smile at least seemed genuine.

"You've been sick?" Doug asked, coming to stand next to Leslie.

Meggy smiled. "Not really sick, Doug, just—well, to be honest, I've been sick every morning."

Doug stared at her blankly, but Leslie understood. "Congratulations." When Doug continued to stare at the two of them, a frown on his face, she said, "Doug, Mrs. Anderson is expecting a baby."

"A baby? Congratulations, Meggy! Ben must be on top of the world! And you're all right?" Doug quickly asked.

"I'm fine." She turned to Leslie. "We've been trying for a few years, so everyone knows about us. It's a small community."

"That's nice. And I'm very happy for you."

"Leslie's living with us," Justin suddenly said, tugging on the other woman's skirt. "And she wants to have babies."

"Justin!" Leslie exclaimed, embarrassed beyond words.

"Son, you shouldn't— That's not—"

"I said, *one day* I'd like to have babies, Justin. Not now. I'm not married, remember?" Leslie hurriedly explained as she recovered from the shock.

"I 'member," Justin agreed solemnly.

"Well, we'd better let Mrs. Meggy start class, boys," Doug suggested with a false heartiness. "We'll be back to pick you up for church."

Doug took Leslie's arm and began leading her down the hallway. She wanted to jerk away, but Meggy's sympathetic smile forced her to pretend to accompany him willingly. As soon as they rounded a corner, she pulled free from him.

"Would you please stop dragging me around?"

"I thought it best to get away from there before my children embarrassed us anymore."

The relief in his voice, echoing her own, startled Leslie and she couldn't hold back a giggle. "They certainly are talented in that respect."

He grinned back and Leslie found herself lost in his brown eyes.

"Yeah. And I haven't even gotten to the teenage years yet."

"I'll pray for you," she promised with a return smile.

He reached out as if to take her hand when someone called out to him.

"My dear Doug! I heard about your accident. How are you?"

"Mrs. Mablethorpe. I'm fine. Jim put it in a cast and I'm back on my feet." Doug took the hand the older woman extended.

"And who is your lovely companion?" the woman asked, a curious look on her face.

"This is Leslie Hibbets, my temporary housekeeper. Leslie, may I present Mrs. Mablethorpe, an old friend of my mother's."

Leslie smiled and extended her hand in spite of the tension she could feel emanating from Doug. "How do you do, Mrs. Mablethorpe."

"Fine, thank you. Are you from the neighborhood? I don't believe I've seen you around." The woman was studying her with a much more critical regard than Meggy Anderson had.

"No, I'm not. I'm from Kansas City."

"Kansas City? A lovely place. I visited it several times. How did you come to work on the Bar-G?"

"Well, I—"

"She was visiting in the area and volunteered her services just until the cast comes off."

Leslie stared at Doug, wondering why he'd stopped her from explaining that she'd answered his ad for a housekeeper.

"So you're staying with the friends you were visiting? Who are they?" Mrs. Mablethorpe stared at Leslie.

Leslie in turn stared at Doug. After all, he's the one who came up with the lie. What was she supposed to answer now?

"She was visiting friends of Dr. Kelsey closer to Cheyenne. He called her and got her to come help out. Moss and the boys love her cooking," Doug offered, awkwardly patting Leslie on the shoulder.

"So you're staying in the bunkhouse?" Mrs. Mablethorpe persisted.

"No, I'm staying in Doug's house. It would be hard to take care of the twins from the bunkhouse." Finally Leslie understood the point of the questions. Mrs. Mablethorpe seemed to have appointed herself the monitor of morals in Riverside. Leslie smiled at her. "The twins are quite adequate chaperons, I can assure you."

"I see," Mrs. Mablethorpe replied with a thin smile. "I'm sure they keep you busy. I'd love to come visit them one day this week. You wouldn't mind, would you?"

"Of course not, if Doug doesn't. In fact, why don't you come to lunch? Tuesday?"

"Lovely. I'll come Tuesday. Thank you, Miss Hibbets." With a gracious nod, she walked down the hall.

"What in the hell do you think you're doing?" Doug whispered harshly in her ear.

"Protecting my reputation. The only way to do that is to invite any and everyone to come visit. Otherwise they'll think we have something to hide." She glared at him as she added in a whisper, "And we don't."

"I know that!" he snapped back.

"Fine!"

"Fine!"

Finally they noticed the stares they were drawing from others passing in the hall.

"Where do we go now?" Leslie whispered, ducking her head.

"The Sunday school class for us is just ahead."

"Us?" she asked, startled.

"Yeah, it's a small church. Everyone under forty meets in the same group."

Oh, great. She was going to have to spend the next hour with him and pretend that his presence had no effect on her. Otherwise, Mrs. Mablethorpe would feel sure she was investigating a den of love next Tuesday.

"This way," Doug said, taking her arm again.

But he dropped it like a red-hot potato when a man about his own age came hurrying up to them.

"Doug! Is this the lady who answered the ad?"

Chapter Ten

Leslie traced a finger down the frozen windowpane as she stared outside. Where was he? As much as Douglas Graybow irritated her, she wanted him safe inside, out of the howling snowstorm that swirled around the house.

"Is Daddy here yet?" Gareth asked, leaning against her legs.

"Not yet. He'll probably be here soon."

"Are you sure we can't open the boxes now? I don't think Daddy would mind. He doesn't like Christmas trees."

Smiling, Leslie tilted Gareth's face up to hers. "I don't think that's true, Gareth. Your father has just been busy. These are his ornaments and I think we should wait for him."

"I think so, too," Justin agreed, joining them at the window. "Daddy seemed disappointed 'cause we couldn't get the tree today."

Leslie was amazed at Justin's perception. She had thought she'd detected regret in Doug's face, also, when, on the way home from church, the snowstorm had moved in, making it impossible to select a tree that afternoon. The cattle had to be tended to, and none of the men had returned.

Their visit to church this morning had been difficult for some reason Leslie didn't understand. He'd been reluctant to introduce her to anyone. And Ben Anderson's question about her responding to the ad had positively infuriated Doug. Though why, Leslie didn't know.

She wouldn't have even met Ben if he hadn't insisted on an introduction. Doug had whispered heatedly to him in response to his question before reluctantly presenting Ben to her. Then he'd rushed her away, and later, in the church service, as soon as the last prayer had been given, he did the same with her and the boys.

As if he was ashamed of her.

Suddenly she could stand the enforced waiting no longer. "Boys, why don't we go down to the barn and muck out the stalls, put out fresh hay for the horses? It will save your dad some work when he gets back."

"Do you know how to do that, Leslie? I thought you lived in a city," Justin asked.

"Well, I know it needs to be done. And I'll have you and Gareth to show me how. Okay?"

Gareth was already heading up the stairs. "I'll be ready before you, Justin," he called, and his brother hurried after him. Leslie followed. At least she wouldn't be standing around worrying all afternoon.

She and the boys packed a snack before they left the warmth of the house. In addition to cookies, she filled a thermos with hot chocolate and one with coffee. When Doug returned, he'd need something warm.

When they stepped outside, the blast of cold air and blinding snow stunned her and made her question her decision. "Boys, should we—I can't see very well."

"Come on, Leslie," Justin said, taking her free hand. "This isn't bad. We can still see the barn."

It was absurd to base her decision on a child's knowledge, but Gareth and Justin knew a lot for five-year-olds. Besides, she couldn't stand waiting another minute in the house.

When they finally reached the safety of the barn, Leslie and the boys shoved the big door behind them and leaned against it to catch their breaths.

"Wow!" Leslie finally said, gasping. "I didn't know it would be that bad. Your father is going to be angry that I let you come out in such a storm."

"No, he won't. Daddy always says a cowboy has to take care of his animals. He'll be proud of you," Gareth said. "Come on. We'll show you what to do."

The next hour was filled with hard work, but Leslie didn't mind. It kept her from thinking about Doug out in the snow. The boys led the horses out of their stalls, tied each one up and then helped Leslie get rid of the old hay and spread out the fresh, clean bundles. Justin would bring a bucket of feed for the animal, Gareth would lead the horse back into the stall and then she and the boys would move to the next one.

When they'd completed the mucking out, the boys asked to go play in the hayloft.

"Does your father let you do that?"

"Sure, Leslie. We've built a fort. Want to come see?"

"No, thanks, Gareth. I think I'll sit here and have a cup of coffee. You be sure to keep your coats on, okay?" she called as the twins scampered off.

Instead of pouring the coffee, she settled back in the nest of fresh hay she'd just spread out in the stall belonging to Doug's horse. After the sleepless night she'd had, even the hay felt comfortable. She'd just close her eyes for a few minutes....

DOUG WAS RELIEVED to see the dim outline of the barn. He'd had to trust Diamond's abilities to get them back safely. The storm was growing worse.

He groaned as he dismounted and opened the barn door. The stables still had to be mucked out. He could leave it for the cowboys, but he wasn't sure they'd get back from town tonight. It wouldn't be the first time they'd had to stay overnight.

At least this work would be sheltered from the storm, even if he wouldn't have a roaring fire to warm by. Once Diamond was inside the barn's sheltering walls, Doug slid the big door closed. Several of the other horses nickered a greeting as he led Diamond to his stall.

Doug greeted some of his animals. When he saw one of them with his nose buried in the feed bin, he paused and looked closer. The stalls had been cleaned.

The cowboys must've gotten back from town. Well, at least he was spared that job. All he had to do was rub down Diamond, and he could return to the house.

He almost missed seeing Leslie as he led Diamond into the stall. In fact, it was Diamond, sniffing the hay, that had Doug looking closer.

"Leslie?" What was she doing out here in the barn? Where were the boys?

She sat up suddenly, giving Diamond a scare. For a couple of minutes, Doug was occupied with his horse.

"Sorry," she said quietly as she rose and stood to one side.

"No problem. What are you doing out here?"

"The boys and I thought we'd help out."

Removing the saddle from Diamond's back, Doug barely took in her answer. Then it occurred to him just what she meant. "You and the boys cleaned out the barn?"

She nodded.

"Why?" he asked gruffly. The woman had cleaned and cooked better than Agnes. She had charmed his boys so they wanted her for their Christmas present. Now she was doing his work for him? What was she, a damned saint? Or a devious woman trying to trap him into marriage?

"Why?" she asked, her voice rising.

"Yeah, why? I could've done it myself."

"Well, excuse me, Mr. Macho Man. I didn't realize I was infringing on your territory. I was just stupid enough to worry about you out in the storm and wanted to keep busy!" She stomped toward the door of the stall.

He only managed to stop her by abandoning Diamond and moving fast. Stepping in her path, he put out a hand to catch her arm, but she jerked away from him.

"Get out of my way. I'm going back to the house."

"Wait, Leslie. I'm sorry."

She turned her head away, clearly not appeased with his apology.

He tried again. "I really appreciate the help."

"Fine," she snapped. When he didn't move, she finally said, "There's coffee and cookies over there if you want them. Assuming you won't accuse me of some dastardly scheme by providing you with a drink." Her stiffness told him he still hadn't been forgiven.

"I'd love a cup of coffee. Would you get it for me while I tend to my horse?" He waited until she moved away from the door before he returned to a patient Diamond.

He removed the bridle and hung it next to the saddle and blanket. Diamond immediately turned to the feed bin. "You fed all the animals?"

"That was Justin's job. Your boys were great. They showed me what to do and worked even harder than me."

"Where are they now?"

"Up in the hayloft, playing in a fort they'd built. That's okay, isn't it?"

"Yeah, if they're warm enough."

"They have hot chocolate and cookies with them."

He'd taken a brush and begun work on Diamond when she stepped to his side with a steaming cup of coffee.

"If you'll tell me what to do, I can work on him while you drink," she suggested.

The need for something hot convinced him. He handed her the brush with a few instructions and took the cup of coffee from her. He stood back in the shadowy dimness of the barn and watched her brush down his horse.

He didn't think he'd ever seen her look sexier. Her tight jeans certainly shaped her cute bottom, and as she stretched to reach different areas, her breasts were outlined in her silhouette. But it wasn't those things that filled him with want.

It wasn't even her silky braid swinging down her back, or the memory of her skin beneath his fingers. Though those things alone would explain the reaction that was tightening his jeans to an uncomfortable state.

What made him want to throw her down into the hay and love her from her toes to the top of her head was her working for him, doing what she didn't have to do, sharing the tough times. Sharing.

Yep, there was a lot of sharing he wanted to do with Leslie Hibbets. But none of it included a wedding ring, he sternly reminded himself. And he wasn't going to seduce her to feed his own wants when he knew he couldn't give her what she wanted. Damn.

"Doug?"

"Hmm?" Her voice drew him from his consuming thoughts and he stepped to her side. "What, Leslie? You tired?"

"No. I wanted to ask you about this morning."

He froze. "What do you mean?"

"Did I do something wrong? You acted as if you were ashamed of me. When your friend, Mr. Anderson, asked about me, I thought you were going to punch him out."

How could he answer her? Yeah, she'd done something wrong. She'd looked like an angel, a very sexy angel, this morning, making him feel he had a lot to ask forgiveness for when he said his prayers. He'd had to hide his response to her in front of his friends. And then Ben had asked about her answering the ad. He'd almost had heart failure.

He didn't want his neighbors to know that she'd answered an ad to be his wife. He'd wanted to protect her from the gossip that knowledge would evoke. Leslie was—was different than he'd imagined those women to be.

"No, you didn't do anything wrong. I just didn't want anyone to get the wrong idea." He set down the almost empty cup and took the brush away from her, letting himself enjoy her warm skin for the briefest of moments.

She stepped aside. "I don't understand."

"I know," he said with a sigh, "and I don't know how to explain." How could he tell her that she was crazy to respond to an ad for a wife, without insulting her? And that's the last thing he wanted to do right now.

"Leslie?" one of the twins called. "Is Daddy back yet? It's getting dark."

"Yes, sweetie," she replied, moving to the door of the stall. "He's rubbing down his horse. Are you ready to go to the house?"

By the time Doug turned around, his boys were there, calling greetings to him. He smiled at them, liking the picture they made with Leslie. She automatically reached out to touch them as they reached her, as if reassuring herself that they were okay.

The boys responded to her touch like little puppies, almost knocking her over to get closer. He knew just how they felt. He'd give anything to forget the rules of good behavior, of honor, to beg for her caresses as his boys felt free to do.

He cleared his throat. "I'm finished. Thanks for the hard work, guys, Leslie. I appreciate it. Now let's get up to the house before we have to spend the night here."

The boys giggled at his words and ran to the door. Leslie looked at him, her eyes wide, as if finally forgiving him for his earlier behavior.

He couldn't help it. He leaned over and kissed her. Breaking it off was hard because her lips were soft and warm, and he could've kissed her forever.

But he did. "Come on," he said, taking her arm. "Let's get to the house."

"UH, THAT WAS a terrific meal." Boy, was that lame. But it was all Doug could think to say when he came back into the kitchen after settling the boys in front of the television. He had managed to avoid Leslie all evening, ever since the kiss in the barn, but now, when they stood in the kitchen cleaning the dinner dishes, he could avoid her no longer.

"You're welcome." She kept her head down, as if amazed by the running water. Then finally she asked, "Would you like to open the boxes of ornaments now?"

"You didn't open them this afternoon? I thought the boys would be entertained with that." That had been his object in mentioning the treasures in the attic. To make up for not getting the tree. After all, he'd promised himself his boys would have a good Christmas.

"Yes, but I thought you'd want to— Never mind. We'll open them tomorrow while you're working." She turned her back to him, appearing to concentrate fiercely on the bowl she was rinsing.

He moved to her side. "Do you want us to open the boxes tonight together?"

She looked at him out of the corner of her eye before turning to the few dishes she had left. "It doesn't matter, but . . . I thought if you told the boys about the ornaments, it would help them appreciate Christmas. The memories are as important as the present, and they don't have many memories."

Since she was kind enough not to mention that his children had *no* memories and it was his fault, he relaxed just a little. "I suppose we could do that. As soon as you're finished we'll start."

Turning off the water, she glanced over her shoulder at him and said in a low voice, "I think you and the boys should open the boxes without me. It's their family memories and has nothing to do with me."

He studied her flushed cheeks before raising his hand to tuck a strand of chestnut-brown hair that had escaped her braid behind her ear. "You have something else you want to do?"

Either his words or his touch startled her and she turned wide blue eyes to look at him. "N-no, but—but this morning you seemed anxious to escape my presence. I don't want to intrude."

Blood flooded his cheeks as shame filled him. She'd been generous to him and his children, worked like a Trojan, and kept a smile on her face even when he'd been difficult. He didn't deserve her kindness. After all, it wasn't her fault that he couldn't keep his hands off her. Was it?

"Leslie, I apologize. It isn't what you think. We'd like to have you join us." Not the most gracious apology he'd ever made, but he hoped she'd accept it.

Some of the tension went out of her, and that incredible smile filled her face. "I'd like that. I have to confess that anything Christmas is magic for me."

He could believe it. Just looking at her filled him with all kinds of magic. "Good. Let's go open those boxes. That program was only for half an hour. The boys should be ready to help us. Unless they're too tired."

She wiped her hands and followed him. "Children don't know the meaning of the word at Christmas."

When they reached the door of the living room, they found evidence of Leslie's words. Instead of watching television, which had been moved back downstairs, the two little boys had one box open and were on their knees beside it, examining something in Justin's hands.

"Well, boys, I see you couldn't wait," Doug said.

"We're sorry," Gareth said, "but we was curious."

"That's okay. What have you found?" Doug wondered if one of his favorite ornaments had been broken.

"We don't know. What is this, Daddy?" Justin extended his hand.

Doug looked at the dried-up piece of greenery and wondered why it had been saved. His mother must have put it in for some special memory.

"Uh, that's mistletoe."

"What do you do with mistletoe?" Justin asked. "Put it on the tree?"

He felt his collar tighten as he saw where the conversation was heading, but he couldn't figure out how to derail it.

"No, you put it ... uh, over doors."

"Why?" Gareth asked, puzzled.

Doug couldn't keep his gaze from Leslie's soft lips as he tried to think of some reason to use mistletoe other than the traditional one.

"It's a Christmas tradition," Leslie said when he hesitated. "See, if you hold it over your head, then I'm supposed to kiss you." She took the mistletoe from Justin and held it over his head. Then she leaned over and kissed his cheek. She did the same to Gareth and then returned it to Justin.

The two boys looked at each other, excitement in their eyes, and Doug groaned. He knew what was coming next.

His boys jumped up and ran to where he'd sat down.

Holding the mistletoe over his head, Justin called, "Come on, Leslie. Come kiss Daddy."

Chapter Eleven

Leslie stared at Justin in shock. She should've expected it, she knew, but somehow she hadn't. Maybe because Justin's order so closely mirrored her own desires, deeply hidden within her. She couldn't admit how much she wanted to be back in Doug's arms. Not when it was impossible. Not when there was no future. Not when—

"Come on, Leslie!" Gareth said impatiently.

"What?" she asked, snapping out of her thoughts.

"Come kiss Daddy."

She fought the warmth she felt in her cheeks, but she knew it was a losing battle. Her dreams had been filled with what they'd shared. Of course, in her dreams, she'd never had an audience of two. "It's the person who's closest who has to do the kissing. You give your father the kiss."

Smiling, she hoped they didn't challenge her newly made-up rule. The disappointment on their faces almost made her laugh, but she wasn't sure she'd avoided an awkward situation just yet.

"Oh. We didn't know that," Justin said, frowning. He bent over and kissed his father's cheek and Gareth did the same. Then they came back to their original places beside the box.

There was a curious silence, but Leslie avoided looking at Doug. She knew he'd be relieved that she hadn't kissed him, but she didn't want to see it. Nor did she want to get any closer to him. As usual, he exuded male toughness, but he also had shown a vulnerability that made her want to take him in her arms.

"Well, shall we look at the Christmas decorations?" she asked brightly.

After waiting all afternoon to reveal the secrets in the cardboard boxes, the two boys put aside the mistletoe and dove in. As they pulled out ornaments carefully packed in tissue, Doug leaned closer, tension evident in his entire body.

It hadn't occurred to Leslie that he might find the unpacking difficult. "These haven't been taken out since your parents died, have they?"

"No." He didn't look at either her or his children. "Mom and Dad went away for a trip to Hawaii just after Thanksgiving. The plane crashed when they were returning."

"The boys and I can do this tomorrow if you'd rather—"

"No," he repeated. "I've run away from good memories for too long." He finally looked at her, his brown eyes dark with emotion. "I need to talk about those good times."

She nodded just as Justin burst into laughter. The tissue he'd opened had revealed a carved dog. "Look. It's a puppy like Santa might bring us."

Doug reached for the ornament and Leslie watched as his fingers caressed the wood. "You probably don't remember our dog, but one of the cowboys carved this for me when I was a kid. It looks just like Rusty."

"Rusty?" Leslie asked. "Why was he named Rusty?"

"Because I liked that name better than Red, and his fur was auburn. I sure couldn't call him that."

"No, I guess not," she agreed with a chuckle.

"What will we name our dog?" Gareth suddenly asked.

"Let's name him Rusty, too," Justin suggested, taking back the ornament from his father and studying it.

"No, I want to name him Skip," Gareth said.

The two boys began to argue, but Doug brought it to an end. "You can't name a dog until you meet him. So we'll just have to wait."

Gareth unwrapped an ornament that was a picture of a baby in a lightweight frame that said Baby's First Christmas. "Who's this?"

"Me."

Both boys turned to stare at their father in fascination and then looked again at the picture.

"You didn't have any hair!" Justin exclaimed.

"Neither did you," Doug told him, grinning.

"Do we have ornaments like this one?" Gareth asked, beginning to dig through the box.

"No, you don't," Doug replied, but Leslie saw the shadows fall over his face.

"But if you have pictures of the twins, I bet you could find an ornament frame for each of them. Then the three of you could hang your ornaments on the tree together." Leslie held her breath, hoping Doug wouldn't dismiss her idea. It seemed important to her that these three be linked together.

"Could we, Daddy?" Justin asked.

"Yeah, I believe we could. Of course I have pictures of you when you were babies. And you look just like I did." Doug reached over and mussed Justin's hair, but his gaze fell on Leslie, and he smiled his thanks.

"Leslie, we'll get one for you. You can put your picture on the tree, too. Then we'll all be on it." Gareth clapped his hands at his idea.

"I don't have a baby picture with me, Gareth. Besides, you should only put the baby pictures of babies born in the family, like you two and your dad."

Neither boy protested but they exchanged another of those looks like the one with the mistletoe. "Then we should get some extra ornament frames in case we have some more babies," Justin said, eyeing his father. "Then we'll be ready."

"Yeah," Gareth agreed with a big smile. "How many should we buy, Daddy?"

Leslie frowned as she watched Doug's cheeks flush as he mumbled an incoherent answer. What was going on? Was Doug planning on marrying soon? She hadn't seen any signs that he was dating. If he was serious about a woman, why wasn't she here caring for him? And holding him?

Fighting down the irritation that filled her, Leslie took a wad of tissue out of one of the boxes and began unwrapping it. She drew in a sharp breath when a small crystal globe emerged. "How beautiful!"

"What is it?" Gareth demanded.

Doug cleared his throat. "It's the first ornament my dad gave Mom. He was promising her the world."

"They must've loved each other very much," she whispered, her gaze focused on the ornament, afraid to look at anyone. They might see the longing she felt. She was afraid her dream was selfish, but she wanted to be the center of a man's universe, as he would be hers.

Somehow she was sure Doug's father had loved his mother that way.

"I like the dog better," Justin said and reached for another ornament.

She couldn't help looking at Doug, afraid his son's cavalier treatment of his memories would hurt him, but he gave her a rueful grin and shrugged his shoulders. Returning his smile, she acknowledged what she'd come to realize the past week. He was a good father... and a good man. He just hadn't spent much time with his children. Maybe it wasn't such a bad thing that he broke his leg.

She felt good about the role she'd played in bringing him and his children together. They were becoming a real family. One that she could finally admit she'd like to be a part of. She loved the twins, in spite of their mischief making. And she was becoming addicted to Douglas Graybow.

His smile brightened the world around her. And when he touched her, he created an entirely new world, one of beauty and excitement. She wanted to be a part of his world.

But he didn't want that.

Unwilling to let the pain spoil the evening for her, Leslie concentrated on making memories. The next hour was a cozy one for her as she listened to Doug talk about his childhood, the teen years, and even touching occasionally on the year his parents died. The boys opened the ornaments and divided them into piles, each claiming the ones he wanted to hang on the tree.

When Doug complained that he and Leslie had none to hang, each boy offered to let one of them help him. Besides, Gareth pointed out, Leslie bought some ornaments at the store the other day. They could hang the new ones.

It was past the boys' bedtime before all the ornaments were unwrapped and divided. Leslie hurried the twins upstairs after a good-night kiss for their dad.

When she came back downstairs a few minutes later, she walked to the door of the living room and discovered Doug still sitting on the floor looking at the ornaments.

"Doug, are you all right?"

Doug hadn't heard Leslie return. He'd been reliving moments in his past that he'd run from the past nine years. Like a coward, he'd tried to shut out the life he'd shared with his parents because their deaths had hurt so much.

In doing so, he'd shut out all emotion. When he'd met Bettina, instead of looking for the love his parents had shared, he'd kept his thoughts on the surface, on his needs, and never considered the important parts of a relationship.

Poor Bettina.

That thought shocked him. He'd always blamed her for their rotten marriage. But now he could even sympathize with Bettina because he'd offered her so little.

"Yeah." He finally answered Leslie's question. His gaze traced her outline as she stood in the doorway, a look of concern on her face. It suddenly occurred to him that he'd told her his life story, and yet he knew almost nothing about her. Abruptly he asked, "Where are your parents?"

Her eyebrows rose but she moved into the room and sat on the edge of the sofa as she answered. "They're both dead. My father was killed in an accident four years ago. My mother was an invalid from the crash and died six months ago.''

"And you're not bitter?" he asked harshly.

She stared across the room at nothing in particular, as if carefully considering her answer. "Bitter? No. If anyone should've been bitter, it would've been Mom. But she never gave in to bitterness."

"She must've been an extraordinary woman," he muttered.

"Yes. Much like your mother, I think. So we've both been lucky."

His head snapped up and he stared at her, surprised. "Lucky? To lose our parents like we did?"

With a gentle smile, she corrected him. "No. Lucky to have had the kind of parents we had. So many children are mistreated, abandoned, unloved. You and I always knew we were loved."

He bowed his head, hiding the strong emotions that ran through him. Yes, he'd always been loved. Unconsciously, perhaps he'd been looking for that unconditional love in Bettina. But he hadn't been willing to risk his heart.

Had he given his children the same security he'd had as a child? He loved them, but did they know? Was it too late to metaphorically wrap his arms around them and never let them face the world alone?

He looked at Leslie again, unable to keep the question from his eyes even if he didn't voice it. Somehow she understood.

"Your boys love you. And they know you love them, too." Then she grinned. "But it wouldn't hurt to spend a little more time with them. After all, I can't break your leg too often without you getting suspicious."

He got up from the floor and crossed to the sofa. Taking her by the hands, he pulled her to her feet. "True. I might realize you were my guardian angel instead of a real person."

"No," she disagreed, smiling at him. "I have too many faults for anyone to think I'm an angel."

"Not from where I'm standing," he whispered, devouring her soft beauty with his gaze. "Thank you for—for bringing back my past for me, Leslie."

"I didn't do anything," she said with a shrug.

But he knew. He knew he'd healed an old wound tonight that would make him happier. And his boys.

Suddenly he lowered his mouth to her soft lips. He heard a faint gasp, but she made no protest. Even as his lips shaped to hers and his arms wrapped around her, he told himself he was only thanking her for the gift she'd given him.

Funny how easy it was to touch her even though he'd promised himself he wouldn't. She fit perfectly in his arms. That was his last conscious thought.

LESLIE ALMOST DROWNED in the sweetness of Doug's kiss. He wasn't groping, pushing, seeking more than she might want to give. His lips molded to hers, and he nestled her against his strong body. The kiss seemed such an extension of the emotions they'd shared the past few minutes that she welcomed the embrace.

Quickly the sweetness changed, grew to a raging hunger that filled her. And felt all too familiar. When he lifted his mouth from hers to stare into her eyes, a burning in his that set off sparks, she realized she was in trouble. Before she could find the words to protest, excuse herself, his mouth covered hers with a fierceness that drew an immediate, uncontrollable answer.

She'd promised herself they wouldn't kiss again. She'd promised herself she wouldn't give in to those fires his touch could start. And, most of all, she'd promised herself that she wouldn't lose her heart to this man.

But they were all empty promises.

She felt his hard body through her clothes and she shuddered. As before, each touch made her desire even more demanding, more overpowering. She pressed against him, wanting more, needing more. Her greediness was so overwhelming that it chased every other thought from her head. She slid a hand over his muscled back and pulled out his shirttail, allowing her to slide her hand underneath his shirt and touch warm skin.

As if she'd given him the idea, Doug burrowed his hands beneath her shirt, caressing, touching, driving her crazy. His mouth slid to her neck, and his hands began unbuttoning her shirt. She kissed his cheek, the stubble she felt only enhancing her response.

Throwing her arms around his neck, she pressed against him, feeling his arousal against her stomach. Her heart leapt with anticipation.

Her action, however, threw Doug off-balance. He took a step backward to steady them, pulling her with him. When glass crunched beneath his boot, Leslie pulled away in surprise.

"What—"

"Doesn't matter," he muttered, reaching for her again.

"Yes!" she panted, reality intruding. "Yes, it matters. What if it was the ornament your father gave your mother?" She parried his reaching hands and looked for the broken glass.

"It wasn't," he assured her, his mouth finding her neck as she bent over.

He was right. It wasn't. But she'd surfaced from her desire long enough to remember that he didn't love her like her father had loved her mother, or his father had loved his mother. In fact, he hadn't said he loved her at all.

And if she didn't stop what was happening right now, the next time she considered her actions would be in the morning, and it would be too late to realize she was making a mistake.

Pulling back, she gasped, "We can't— Stop, Doug. We can't do this."

"Why not?" he growled, his lips honing in on hers once more.

She knew why. She knew a million reasons why. But the most important one was that he didn't love her. Shoving him away, she said, "You don't love me."

He froze before turning and stomping away from her. "You want me to say the magic words, like please and thank you? Is that it?"

"No," she said, fighting the sob in her throat. "I don't want you to say anything you don't mean. But— but I can't sleep with you just because—I can't." She turned and ran for the door.

"Leslie!"

Should she stop, respond? No. Only that word was clear. No. She had to save herself. Because if she'd stayed in his embrace much longer, she would never want to leave. And she was the temporary housekeeper, the one he hadn't wanted and planned to send on her way as soon as the cast was removed. The one he didn't love.

She raced up the stairs to her bedroom, closing the door behind her, frantically looking for a way to block the entrance since there was no lock. She came to her senses as she began to shove a chair across the room.

"What is wrong with you?" she asked herself, straightening to listen. There was no sound of pursuing footsteps. The house was silent.

"Of course not," she muttered. Doug wasn't an animal. Only a man who wouldn't resist temptation. And she had tempted him. Oh, she knew he initiated the kiss. But even now she could remember its sweetness. Somehow it had changed, though, and she wasn't sure whose fault that was. She certainly hadn't resisted the second kiss, so different from the first.

That kiss had spoken of hunger, raging need, desire. Not exactly appropriate for the housekeeper. Unless Douglas Graybow thought he'd add a few duties to her job description.

What should she do now? She should put the chair under the doorknob to keep herself in her room. Except, of course, that wouldn't work. Should she leave? She couldn't do that. The boys wouldn't understand, and she'd promised them a Christmas to remember. She'd given her word.

Was she making excuses because she wanted to stay? Because, secretly, she hoped Doug would give her reasons to stay... forever?

She sank down on the bed. That was it. And it was about time she admitted the truth: In spite of her warnings to herself, she'd fallen in love with him.

DOUG STOOD PARALYZED where Leslie had left him. He hadn't been with a woman in so long, he was shocked by how quickly he'd lost control. And it happened every time he touched Leslie.

If she hadn't stopped him, he knew he would have carried their embrace to its logical conclusion. He laughed derisively at himself. Logical conclusion. Such a dry description of the raging, burning passion that had swept through him.

What now? Was she going to storm out of the house, infuriated that he'd attacked her? He remembered her first night, when she'd accused him of pawing her. She'd certainly been on her way out then. And he'd taken the pawing a bit further this evening. In fact, he'd practically eaten her alive.

He stood there, listening, waiting for her to come back down the stairs. What would he do if she tried to leave? He couldn't force her to stay. But he wanted to. He had the urge to lock her in a room and not let her out until she promised—promised what? To warm his bed each night? The idea brought a resurgence of the tension that had been slowly easing.

He thought he'd lusted after Bettina. That desire didn't even begin to compare to what Leslie stirred. Why? She wasn't that much prettier. It suddenly occurred to him that the difference might be Leslie's heart.

She had a big heart. His boys would be safe in her care. *He* would be safe in her care. Of course, he didn't love her, but he could marry her, he suddenly realized. He could marry her and solve all his problems.

His boys would have a terrific mother. He would have a woman in his bed who stirred his senses. There might even be more babies, as his sons wanted. And Leslie would never demand anything. She was too good, too wonderful, too giving.

He began to pace the room, deep in thought. He'd explain what he wanted, and she'd agree. After all, that's why she came in the first place, wasn't it? To marry him. And she already loved his boys, and he didn't think he repulsed her. A smile covered his face as he relived her response. No, he didn't repulse her. Even when she pushed away, she'd been reluctant to release him.

That thought pleased him. Yeah, she wouldn't object to their sleeping together. As long as they were married. And once he proposed, maybe she'd be willing— He halted his thoughts as his body began to respond. Many more of these thoughts and he'd be in a cold shower all night.

With a firm nod, he spun on his heel and headed for the stairs, confident that he'd just solved all his problems. This marriage wouldn't be like the last one. He wouldn't promise to love her, to make himself vulnerable to her. He'd just marry her. That would satisfy Leslie, and the thought of her in his bed promised satisfaction to him very soon.

Everything was going to work out just fine.

EVEN THOUGH THE BOYS had gotten to bed an hour past their bedtime, they were up and trying to rouse Leslie shortly after six.

"Leslie? Are you sick?" Justin asked, patting her shoulder.

She opened one eye and then groaned. "No, I'm not sick. I fell asleep late last night." Very late. She'd tossed and turned for hours.

"Are you going to get up? We're hungry," Gareth said.

"Yes, I'm going to get up and have a shower. Why don't you two go down and have some cereal? You can eat it in the living room and watch cartoons as long as you don't use milk."

"Really?" Gareth asked in surprise.

"Really. I'm going to take a shower, and I'll fix you some more breakfast after I'm dressed."

Much to her relief, the novelty of eating their cereal in front of the television had the boys racing down the stairs. After a moment of silence, she slid out of bed and gathered clean clothes before heading for the shower. She only hoped the hot water would wash away the cobwebs in her brain. And the soreness in her heart.

Several hours later, she was sitting on the couch in the living room folding a fresh load of laundry as the boys watched "Sesame Street" when she heard Doug's footsteps coming down the stairs. Immediately she froze.

She sat stiffly, listening to him walk into the kitchen and then turn around and come down the hall. Her breathing grew shallow and she noticed her palms were damp. How would he behave? Would *he* want *her* to leave? That thought hadn't occurred to her before, and it almost took her breath away.

"Good morning," Doug sang out, a cheerful smile on his face that surprised Leslie.

The boys jumped up from the floor and ran to hug their father. Just as quickly, they returned to their places to stare at the television.

Leslie forced herself to return to the folding of the towel in her lap. After one quick look, she avoided meeting Doug's gaze. "There's some bacon and toast on the back of the stove if you want it. You can heat it in the microwave."

She'd figured she could avoid being alone with him if she already had some breakfast ready.

"Aren't you going to heat it for me?"

His question, asked as if he were teasing her, drew her gaze. He met her look with a warm smile, and she blinked several times, unable to believe her eyes. Then she frowned. What was he up to?

"Boys, you don't mind if I borrow Leslie for a few minutes to fix my breakfast, do you?"

He received a wave of Justin's hand. Gareth slowly nodded. Neither turned around. Bert and Ernie were arguing about sharing their room and the boys were interested in the outcome.

Her gaze returned to him. "You can punch the buttons on the microwave as well as I can."

His brown eyes darkened and Leslie shivered.

"I need to talk to you," he assured her.

She'd been right. He was going to ask her to leave. Or try to convince her to expand her duties to his bedroom. Either one meant she'd be packing her bags. Stiffly she got to her feet and walked past him without a word.

When he closed the kitchen door behind him, Leslie was leaning against the sink, bracing herself for the worst. Promising herself she wouldn't cry.

"Look, Leslie, about last night," he began. Then he paused, as if waiting to see if she had anything to say, but she didn't. "I—I hope I didn't offend you when I kissed you." Again he paused. She remained still and silent as a statue. "I guess you can tell I'm attracted to you."

She closed her eyes briefly. He was going to ask her to be his mistress. If she'd had a butcher knife at hand, she might've buried it in his heart.

"I've come up with a solution to our problem."

"I don't want to hear any more. I'll pack my bags," she said, pushing away from the counter and heading toward the door.

He caught her by the arm. "Wait. I haven't finished."

"I won't sleep with you, Doug. That's not part of a housekeeper's duties."

"No, but it's part of a wife's duties. Though I hope you won't consider it a duty."

The idiot was grinning at her. What was he talking about?

"Leslie? Don't you understand? I'm asking you to marry me."

Chapter Twelve

Like a flash point, joy raced through Leslie. She hadn't realized how much she'd longed to hear those words until he actually said them.

Almost as quickly, the joy dissipated. Something was wrong with her storybook dream. The hero wasn't overcome with passion, sweeping her into his arms, promising her his love and devotion. No, Douglas Graybow was standing there grinning at her as if he'd just told a joke.

"Why?"

Her simple question wiped the grin away. "Why?" he repeated. "It makes good sense. I'll admit I didn't think it would when you first arrived, but I agree now."

"What are you talking about?"

"Our getting married. Aren't you awake yet?" he teased, his grin returning.

"You're asking me to marry you because it makes good sense? Because it would solve your problems with baby-sitting, cooking, cleaning, someone to sleep with?" Her blood was beginning to boil, but Doug seemed to have no clue to her emotions.

"That's right. You already love the boys. And last night, if not before, we proved that we're not immune to each other, either. It all makes good sense, like I said."

She turned to walk away, afraid of what she'd say, but he caught her arm and pulled her to a stop. "Where are you going? You haven't answered my proposal yet."

If his expression was anything to go by, he was surprised by the glare she sent him. "My answer is no!"

"Why? Maybe I didn't explain it right, Les, but it makes good sense. You like it here. You can't tell me you wouldn't like to stay."

"My wanting to stay has nothing to do with your—your cockamamy marriage proposal." She spat out each word.

"Why are you upset? And what's wrong with my proposal?" He was losing the insouciance he'd shown earlier.

"You don't know what's wrong with your proposal?" she raged. "You offer me a—a marriage without heart, a legal joining so you won't have to pay my wages, and you ask what's wrong with it? How dare you!"

"How dare I?" he raged in return. "What's so different about this proposal than the one you wanted when you first came? Tell me that!"

"What are you talking about?"

"You came here in answer to that stupid ad, and now you're complaining because I'm doing exactly what you expected me to do. Women!"

"I expected you to hire me as a housekeeper. I don't know what *you're* talking about." Again she turned to leave the room.

What was she saying? He was so confused, he could barely react. "Don't be ridiculous. That ad was a month old. You answered the ad for a wife."

She turned around, a horrified look on her face. "What?"

"I said you came here to be my wife, and now you're—"

"You advertised for a wife?"

"No, *I* didn't! Ben and another guy thought they'd help me and they put the ad in without my knowledge." He shoved his hand through his blond hair and stared at her, incredulous. "You mean you really came here for a housekeeping job?"

"Of course I did. I would never— You thought I just showed up on your doorstep thinking you'd marry me? How absurd!"

"You wouldn't think so if you'd seen the responses I got in the mail. Some of those pictures were definitely X-rated."

They stared at each other as what had been revealed settled in their heads. Leslie didn't know what to say. She was stunned that all this time he'd thought she was—was trying to get him to marry her.

"Look, Les, I'm sorry. I thought— But even if you didn't come in answer to the ad, my marriage idea still is a good one."

His brown eyes were warm, sincere, but they weren't burning brightly with love. It was easier to reject his proposal when she could work up a good head of steam. Even so, it had to be rejected.

"No, I'm sorry, Doug, but I can't." She turned away, unable to face him.

"Why not?"

"Because I intend to have a marriage like my parents had. A marriage where spending time together is more important than anything else in the world. Where I'm the center of my husband's universe and he's the center of mine. Not a business arrangement for everyone's convenience."

She hurried from the kitchen.

Doug stared after her in frustration. Women! He'd never understand them. Why couldn't they be reasonable like Moss or Curly? If he'd been talking to one of the men, he could have explained what he wanted and they'd accept it.

Or argue with him, he admitted. But they wouldn't run away in tears.

Damn it, he'd thought all his problems would be solved when he proposed. Now what was he going to do?

It was a damn shame. Leslie was a fine woman and would make an excellent mother. She was no slouch in the kissing department, either.

He should've known better. Women liked everything wrapped up in candy and flowers. But Leslie was such a reasonable woman. He thought she'd understand.

When his cast came off, she'd leave and he'd have to start looking for a housekeeper all over again.

Doug stopped and frowned. Why would he have to do that? Leslie wanted a job as a housekeeper. He needed one. Why couldn't she just stay on permanently?

Of course, he'd prefer that she share his bed, but he was sure he could control his impulses. Couldn't he? He hadn't managed that well recently, but now that he knew how she felt, he could keep from touching her. Maybe he'd start dating again, find someone else to kiss.

He just knew he couldn't lose Leslie. She had become too important to him—to his boys, he meant.

Yeah. She was too important to his boys. They needed Leslie to stay.

Who was he kidding? *He* needed Leslie to stay. Even if she wouldn't sleep with him. Just for a while, until he and the boys were able to manage. Just a little while longer.

Having resolved everything to his satisfaction once more, he rushed up the stairs to tell Leslie. He came to an abrupt stop at her doorway when he saw the suitcase open on the bed.

"What are you doing?"

She didn't even look over her shoulder. "I'm packing."

"Why?"

"I think it's best that I leave."

"Best for whom? Not for me or the boys. You promised them a great Christmas. What are you going to tell them?"

She turned around to face him. "Doug, surely you can't expect me to stay here after what was just said in the kitchen?"

"Of course I can. You promised you'd stay until the cast came off. As far as I can tell, it's still on." He stuck out his leg for emphasis.

"This is ridiculous. It would be too awkward—"

"No, it wouldn't. We both know I was—was proposing as a matter of convenience. No emotions were involved. No hurt feelings, so I don't see why you can't stay. In fact..." He paused and studied her face. "In fact," he repeated, licking his suddenly dry lips, "I don't see why you can't stay permanently. If you came here for a job, and I need to hire someone, why not stay?"

Her mouth dropped open. Then she snapped it shut and glared at him. "No. I can't do that."

"Why not?"

"I've changed my mind. I'm going home as soon as that stupid cast comes off."

He'd taken a couple of steps toward her, but he backed away. She looked as if she wanted to kick his broken leg. "Les, I don't understand. Why are you upset?"

"Just go away and leave me alone, Douglas Graybow, and don't even think of discussing this subject ever again!"

Doug went.

He remained hidden in his office the rest of the morning, trying to concentrate on the ranch accounts but not having much luck. Everything had gone haywire that morning, and he couldn't figure out where he'd gone wrong. But because he had, Leslie was going to leave as soon as she could.

He didn't want to admit how much that thought bothered him. How empty the house would feel without her.

In spite of her last warning, he couldn't help but hope he could change her mind by the time Christmas rolled around. He'd just have to work on it.

After a subdued lunch, he offered to take the boys down to the bunkhouse with him so Leslie could have some time to herself. She stiffly thanked him and helped the boys bundle up. Clearly she wanted none of their company.

Holding each boy's hand, he set out in the snow for the company of other men.

"What's wrong with Leslie?" Justin asked.

"What?"

"Leslie seems unhappy. I think she's been crying."

Doug looked sharply at his son. "Why do you say that?"

"I heard her sniffin'."

"Me, too," Gareth added. "I asked her, but she said she was catching a cold."

"Could be," Doug said. "But women—women just cry sometimes. Who can say why?"

They plodded in the snow in silence until Justin asked, an accusing note in his voice, "Did you make her sad?"

Doug had never been taken to task by his twins before, and he didn't like the feeling. "If I did, I didn't do it on purpose."

He received several covert glances from the boys but they said nothing else. The walk to the bunkhouse had never seemed so long.

When they finally entered the building, Doug released their hands and walked to the stove to pour himself a cup of coffee. "Hi. Everyone get back all right?"

"We're fine. Sorry about not making it back last night," Moss said.

Doug assured his foreman there was no problem and then joined his men around the big table and discussed men topics—weather, cows, trucks—things he could understand.

Justin sidled up next to Moss and tapped him on the shoulder. "We need to talk to you," he whispered.

Moss looked surprised, but he nodded and slipped away from the table while a vigorous discussion about vehicle preferences ensued. He walked to the door leading into the sleeping area, and the two boys followed.

"What is it, boys?" he asked, sitting down on the edge of a bunk.

"Have you ever heard of mistletoe?" Gareth asked.

"Why, sure. It's fine stuff," Moss said with a grin.

"Do you know what you're supposed to do with it?" Justin asked in hushed tones.

"You're supposed to kiss the first little lady you find near it." Moss looked at the two of them. "You two been kissing the ladies?"

"No," Justin said, ignoring his teasing. "Can you get us some?"

"Mistletoe? Well, I reckon so," Moss said, scratching his chin.

"And we'll need some help putting it over the doors, too," Gareth added.

"I suppose I could help you there, too. But we might ought to take care of that when your dad's not there. Sort of let it be a surprise to him and Leslie, right?"

The boys beamed, glad their friend understood.

The three of them returned to the main room and settled back around the table. In a few minutes, Moss found himself in demand again.

"Uh, Moss, I need to speak to you. Boys, you stay here with Curly." Doug motioned to the sleep room.

Moss followed. "Yeah? Something wrong, Doug?"

"I just wondered if you'd heard of anyone with puppies for sale in the neighborhood."

"You gonna buy a dog?"

"Leslie thought the boys should get a dog for Christmas."

"Good idea. I heard the Martins' Lab had a litter a week or two ago, but they may have promised them all."

"A Lab? Oh, yeah, I remember that dog. Well behaved. Maybe I'll give 'em a call right now." Doug moved to the phone, looked up the number in the directory and dialed.

When he hung up the phone a couple of minutes later, he was grinning. "They've promised two, but there are four more. I told 'em we'd be over this afternoon to choose one."

"We? Who's we?"

Doug felt his cheeks redden, but he tried to act nonchalant. "I thought Leslie should get to help choose the dog since it was her idea. Could I leave the boys here for an hour or two? Oh, and we want to keep the dog a secret."

"You bet. The boys and I have a few things to do anyway. Take all the time you want."

Doug barely took the time to explain to the boys that he had an errand to run and they were to stay with Moss before he was crossing the distance between the bunkhouse and home. He only hoped he could persuade Leslie to come with him.

"Leslie?" he called as he stamped the snow from his boots.

"Yes?" she answered calmly, sticking her head out the kitchen door.

"You busy?"

"Just cleaning."

"I've found some puppies. Can you come with me to pick one out?" He watched as she considered her answer.

"I really should stay here and clean."

"Come on, Leslie. They've got four. I'll never be able to choose. And this was all your idea." He moved a few steps closer.

"Someone has to take care of the boys. I should stay here."

"Moss is in charge of the terrible twins this afternoon. I think they're planning a surprise for us, for Christmas, you know. They'll be fine." He didn't care what they were doing. It seemed important to him to get Leslie alone with him, in the truck, where she couldn't run away.

"All right, if we hurry," she finally agreed. "I'll go get my coat."

As she turned and went up the stairs, Doug let out a long breath. If they could just get past the awkwardness Leslie seemed to feel about what had happened this morning, maybe she'd reconsider.

Surely picking out a puppy would be something she'd enjoy, something they could do together.

LESLIE GLARED AT DOUG. "How could you possibly think that puppy is the cutest? This little fellow is perfect."

She snuggled the chocolate-brown lab puppy against her cheek and Doug felt his mouth go dry. He tried to concentrate on the subject at hand—the puppy—instead of on Leslie's lips.

"But he's the runt of the litter, Leslie. This guy is big and strong. I want a dog to protect you when I'm in the saddle."

"Oh, pooh! He'll grow, won't you, sweetie?" she crooned to the puppy, which licked her face in return. "Aren't you just the sweetest thing? I know the boys would prefer this puppy, Doug."

Mr. Martin had been watching them with a grin on his face, but Doug didn't care. At least Leslie wasn't being stiff and silent as she had in the truck on the drive over. Just as he was about to give in to Leslie's choice, the man spoke.

"Seems to me you ought to get a puppy for each boy. Then the puppies wouldn't get lonely at night, and each boy would have his own dog."

Leslie's blue eyes lit up and she turned to Doug, really looking at him for the first time. "Could we, Doug? Could we get two puppies?"

She could've asked for the world at that moment and he wouldn't have said no. Fortunately, she was only asking for two dogs.

"We could do that. In fact, I think it's a real good idea. How much for two, Bud?" He didn't really care about the price. It would be worth whatever it cost for the look on Leslie's face.

"I'll give you a deal. Three hundred for both of them. I've been asking two hundred apiece, but after all, we're friends."

"I appreciate it. You've got a deal."

Leslie was tugging on his arm as he extended it to Bud Martin. "We don't really have to have two dogs, Doug. I was being silly."

He frowned at her. What was she up to now? "I want two dogs, Leslie. I think each boy should have his own dog. Now if you don't want the runt of the litter, just say so, but otherwise we've bought ourselves two dogs."

She cuddled the puppy closer to her, a dismayed look in her eye. "Couldn't we just buy this one?"

"Nope. So let's buy both of them. Okay?"

She nodded and turned away. He pulled out his checkbook and wrote a check for the dogs. "Can we leave them here until Christmas Eve? You're not going out of town, are you?"

"Naw, we'll be here. And we'll be up late putting together a danged bicycle. Just come by anytime."

"Thanks. Leslie, give the man back his puppy. We'll come get them Christmas Eve."

"You won't forget which ones we want?" she asked, worry in her voice.

"No, ma'am. I won't forget." The man grinned at her and Leslie managed a smile in return.

Once they were in the truck and headed back to the ranch, Leslie said, "Doug, I'll be glad to pay for the little one. You only intended to buy one."

"Don't be silly, Leslie. Once Bud suggested it, it seemed like the perfect solution to me."

"But they're very expensive."

"Is that what was bothering you? The cost?" He shook his head in disgust. "Leslie, I'm not bankrupt. I can afford to buy my boys Christmas presents."

"I just thought— Never mind." She turned her face toward the window, away from him.

Since she wasn't looking, he reached over and picked up her hand. She jumped as if he'd attacked her.

"That's sweet of you, honey, but it's not necessary. Okay?"

"Don't." She pulled her hand from his and kept her face averted.

"Don't what? Don't talk to you? Don't appreciate your offer? What?"

"Don't—don't hold my hand." Her cheeks were red.

He pulled the truck off to the side of the road. "Leslie, we've got to work this out. You can't avoid me if you're living in my house, cooking for me, taking care of my kids. You've at least got to look at me."

"I have," she assured him, staring out the window.

"Once, when you were pleading for that runt of a puppy."

She turned around then, flashing her eyes at him. "Don't call him a runt. He's—he's just a late bloomer."

"A late bloomer? Come on, Leslie, he's—a late bloomer," he suddenly agreed with a grin. The fire in her eyes convinced him.

His reward was a tentative smile. "Thanks."

"Friends?"

She licked her lips before she answered and his gut tightened. The desire to taste those lips again, as he had last night, almost consumed him. "Friends. But I don't want what happened last night to— I mean, it mustn't happen again."

"I didn't intend it to happen last night. I just wanted to say thank-you. I'm sorry things got out of hand." He couldn't bring himself to promise it wouldn't happen again. But he'd try.

She nodded, then looked ahead. "We'd better hurry. Moss seems to go crazy if he's left with the twins for too long."

"You're right. I wonder what they were planning."

"HERE?" MOSS ASKED in exasperation, staring down at his two directors.

"Yes, there," Justin agreed.

"Are you sure?" Gareth asked.

"He's sure. I ain't movin' it again, you ornery cusses. When your daddy comes through the door and sees what we've done, I'll be in enough trouble without having aching arms." Moss tapped in the tack holding the mistletoe and climbed down from the kitchen chair.

"I think he'll like it," Gareth said. "And we put up lots and lots."

"That we did. Leslie can't go through any door in the house without passing under one of those kissin' traps."

"Will Leslie like it?" Justin asked, suddenly worried.

"Who knows, boy? Women are even ornerier than you two. Just act innocent, tell her you were decoratin' for Christmas, like you don't know any different. That'll work."

"Okay. Did you know we're going to get Leslie for Christmas?" Gareth asked.

"Gareth! You weren't supposed to tell!" Justin protested.

"What are you talkin' about?" Moss asked, his gaze sharpening on the boys.

"We're asking Santa if we can have Leslie for our mommy. And if Santa won't bring her, then we're going to beg Daddy to marry her. That's why they need to kiss. That's what people do on television," Gareth explained.

"I hear the truck," Justin shouted, rushing to the window. "It's them."

He ran for the kitchen chair and dragged it down the hall to the kitchen. Before the door opened, he was back and he and his brother pulled Moss into the living room.

When Doug and Leslie came into the house, the sound of the television told them the twins were there.

"Boys?" Leslie called out.

"In here," Gareth replied.

Leslie stepped to the door of the living room, Doug right behind her, to find both boys and Moss standing there, grinning at them.

Before she could greet them, the boys started shouting at their father and pointing above their heads.

Leslie's gaze went up and there, right over her head, was a big batch of mistletoe.

Chapter Thirteen

"Kiss her, Daddy, kiss her!" Doug's sons shouted, dancing around him and Leslie.

As much as Doug wanted to taste her lips, he couldn't forget how upset she'd been when he'd touched her hand. If he wanted Leslie to stay, he'd better pay attention to what she wanted. Besides, her wide-eyed stare, panic in her eyes, would've stopped him cold in any circumstances.

He leaned over and kissed her cheek. "Merry Christmas, Leslie." Then, as if nothing had happened, as if her soft skin beneath his lips had meant nothing, he turned to Moss. "How'd it go, Moss? The boys give you any trouble?"

There was a curious silence as Moss and both boys looked from him to Leslie and back again.

"Moss?"

"Uh, everything went fine. The boys wanted to do a little decorating for Christmas. Hope you don't mind." Moss looked a little anxious, and Doug didn't blame him.

"Of course not," Leslie replied, since Moss was watching her. "I'm glad the boys are enthusiastic about the holidays."

All four males seemed to breathe a little easier at Leslie's calm response. At least Doug knew he did. "Yeah, that's great, boys."

Leslie turned to leave the room, and Gareth grabbed her hand. "Where are you going, Leslie?"

"To hang up my coat, Gareth. Why?"

"We're hungry, that's why," Justin quickly said.

Doug watched Leslie respond to his son's comment like the calvary hearing a bugle horn sound the charge. Immediately her attention turned to feeding them.

"How about some hot chocolate and a cupcake? I baked some while you were at the bunkhouse today." After the boys' eager agreement, she took them by the hand and started for the kitchen.

"Uh, Leslie, does that offer extend to big boys?" Moss asked.

She grinned at him and nodded. Her gaze traveled to Doug and her grin wavered a little, but she kept it in place. "There's plenty," she added, before leaving the room.

Doug started to follow, but Moss caught him by the arm.

"I think I should warn you, this isn't the only door with mistletoe over it."

"Oh?" Doug raised one eyebrow and waited for more information.

"Uh, yeah. The boys got a little carried away. We, uh, we put it over a few more doors." Moss was avoiding his gaze, and Doug knew he wasn't getting the complete picture.

"Just how many more doors?"

Moss cleared his throat. "All of them."

"All?"

Moss nodded solemnly. "The boys wanted to be sure you got in a lot of kisses. They're planning on a mama for Christmas."

"I know," Doug informed his manager with a weary grin. "But that's not going to happen. Leslie didn't come here in answer to the ad for a wife. She saw the old ad, the one for a housekeeper."

Moss's stunned look almost made Doug grin. Almost.

"Really?" Moss asked, as if he couldn't believe his ears. Then he shook off his amazement and clapped Doug on the shoulder. "Well, that don't mean you should give up. She's a fine woman. But, hell, boss, that namby-pamby kiss on the cheek won't cut the mustard."

Doug's cheeks stung with color. "I didn't want to embarrass her," he muttered.

"Next time—"

Moss's instruction was interrupted by Gareth's appearance in the doorway. "Come on, Daddy, Moss. Leslie has your cupcakes ready."

Doug willingly answered the summons. He didn't need Moss telling him how to kiss Leslie. He'd already discovered several times over that he had a special talent for kissing her.

They entered the kitchen and sat down. Leslie had poured two cups of steaming coffee and put a plate of cupcakes in the center of the table.

"Aren't you having anything, Leslie?" he asked as she headed for the door.

"No, I'm not hungry. I'm going to go freshen up while you eat."

As soon as she was out the door, the boys abandoned their cupcakes to get on their knees and lean across the table.

"Daddy! That's not how you're supposed to kiss her," Justin whispered urgently.

"We saw it on television, Daddy," Gareth explained. "You're supposed to put your arms around her and kiss her on the lips."

Getting instructions from another man was embarrassing, but having your children direct your love life was appalling. Doug shook his head and explained, "I don't think Leslie would like that."

"The ladies on television always do," Gareth assured him.

"Yeah, they kiss a long time," Justin agreed. "They wouldn't do that if they didn't like it."

"I agree," Moss said, drawing a glare from Doug. "I think if you'd try it once, you'd both like it a lot."

Damn. How was he going to get out of this situation? He couldn't explain that he'd already tried kissing Leslie and had liked it so much, he'd proposed marriage this morning. Because then he'd have to tell the boys she turned him down. And he couldn't kiss her, as they suggested, because she'd pack her bags and leave.

"See, Daddy? If you'll just stand by the door and call Leslie, she'll come down and you can kiss her on the lips," Justin explained, his look of determination almost comical except that it was creating problems for his father.

"Okay," he agreed slowly, trying to think of a diversion. Finally he said, "I'd better go brush my teeth. I think I have bad breath, and Leslie wouldn't like that."

His boys, television watchers, agreed immediately, having discovered, via television commercials, that bad breath was a terrible thing. Doug avoided Moss's eyes as he rose from the table, but he could feel the astonishment he was sure was on Moss's face.

Once away from the kitchen, Doug hurried up the stairs and rapped on Leslie's door.

"Yes?" she called.

"Les, I have to talk to you."

She opened the door, surprise on her face. "What's wrong?"

He pointed to the sprig of green above the door. "Did you notice that?"

Taking a step back, she glared at him. "You knocked on my door to catch me under the mistletoe? How juvenile can you get, Doug?"

"Look, Leslie, I have a problem and I'm asking for some help. Will you listen to me?"

She nodded, but he noticed she kept her distance.

"The boys are waiting for you to come back into the kitchen, over which door you'll also find mistletoe. They expect me to kiss you, and they've given specific instructions that the kiss should be on the lips this time."

"You're making this up, Doug. I'm ashamed of you."

"I am not!" he protested, frustration rising in his voice. "You tell me what to do. Because I sure as hell can't figure it out. If I disappoint them, they'll continue to pester me to kiss you. If I do, you'll pack your bags and hightail it out of here. So what do I do, Miss Brains?"

Leslie stared at him in dismay. If he was telling the truth, and she had to admit the plan sounded exactly like something the boys would dream up, they'd never leave them alone until they saw them kiss. On the lips.

Confused and frustrated, she reached for her top button to twist it as she had always done when she was trying to think.

"What are you doing?" Doug asked harshly.

She frowned at him. "Trying to think of an answer to your question. What do you think?" she retorted.

"You're not—you're not unbuttoning your shirt?"

Now she was really confused. She stared at him. "Unbuttoning my shirt? Why would I do that?"

"That first night, you reached for your top button."

She shrugged, puzzled by his pursuit of a silly topic. "I twist my button when I'm thinking. Does it bother you?" Then the meaning of his question hit her. "You thought I was undressing?"

He nodded. "After those pictures I'd received from the women who—who wanted to marry me, nothing would have been a surprise."

She stood there, her mouth open, stunned by what he'd said. He, however, recovered more quickly.

"Leslie, I have to go back down. What are we going to do?"

"All I can think of is for us to—to kiss as if it means nothing. If we refuse, the boys will get upset. If we kiss like—like lovers, they'll think you're going to marry me. But if we kiss as if we were saying hello, they won't get their hopes up."

He gave her a look she couldn't interpret, nodded and hurried to the stairs. She collapsed against the doorjamb and covered her mouth with her hand. What had she just agreed to? If she could carry this off, she'd deserve an Academy Award.

Treat Doug's kisses as if they meant nothing, as if they didn't affect her? Yeah, right. And in front of an audience, too.

She turned back into her room, hoping to compose herself, but one of the boys called from downstairs.

"Leslie?"

"I'll be right down." Of course she would. It was her job. She only hoped she survived it.

When she entered the kitchen, Doug was standing by the door.

"Leslie, look at the surprise the boys made," he said and pointed to the sprig of mistletoe over the door. "Merry Christmas," he murmured and then pulled her into his arms.

She hadn't counted on his holding her. As his strength pressed against her, she gasped, and his lips covered hers. She felt her arms go around his neck and willed them back to her side. But they didn't listen. She told her eyes to stay open, but her lids grew heavier than she could bear. She ordered her lips not to cling to his. They ignored her.

The next thing she knew, Doug was setting her away from him and the boys were cheering.

"Is that the way it should be done?" Doug demanded with laughter, turning to look at his sons, blocking her vision of them. Then he turned back to her, after his sons assured him he'd performed perfectly, and, with a warning look in his eyes, said, "Well, Leslie, I told you we could convince them. You see, boys, while I was upstairs, I explained to Leslie how disappointed you were. She thought we should kiss the way you wanted for Christmas."

The boys' gazes immediately flew to her.

"You mean you didn't like it?" Justin asked, horrified.

"Um, yes, I mean, no, I did like it," Leslie stammered, caught off guard. "I mean, people kiss like that at Christmas. It doesn't mean anything."

The boys looked at each other in disappointment and Leslie thought she'd scotched their plan. Until Moss spoke.

"I don't know," the foreman muttered, as if seriously considering the situation. "I think with practice you could get better."

"Practice?" Leslie squeaked.

"Better?" Doug demanded, in strangled tones.

"Yeah, that's it," Gareth agreed, nodding his head vigorously. "You just need to practice."

Moss coughed and Leslie could have sworn he was hiding a grin behind his big hand. "Well, now that that's settled, I'd better get back to the bunkhouse. It's been a fun afternoon," he assured all of them, but Leslie noticed he didn't meet her gaze. Or Doug's.

"He gets to ride fence tomorrow," Doug muttered after the cowboy left, and then met Leslie's gaze.

If he'd been triumphant, even teasing, she would've killed him, but there was an apology in his gaze, even though she knew what had happened wasn't his fault.

With a smile, she said in return, "Good," and began clearing the table.

"But, Daddy, I thought Moss hated riding fence," Justin said, a frown on his face.

"He does, son, but sometimes you have to do things you hate. It's all part of life."

"Oh." Seemingly satisfied with his father's explanation, Justin offered Leslie his help in tidying up the kitchen.

When they were finished, Leslie told the boys to go put together a new puzzle she'd bought them while she was in town.

"What are you going to do?" Gareth asked.

"I'm going to start preparations for my luncheon."

"But lunch isn't until tomorrow," Gareth pointed out.

"I know, sweetie, but I'm having company for lunch tomorrow. You two will have to be on your best behavior."

Doug groaned. "I forget Mrs. Mablethorpe is coming to lunch. I wanted us to get the Christmas tree tomorrow."

The boys jumped up and down at their father's idea, but Leslie shook her head. "Not until after she leaves, I'm afraid. I want everything running smoothly."

"You sure you're up for this?" Doug asked.

"Of course," Leslie replied, holding back hysterical laughter. Fixing lunch for a thousand Mrs. Mablethorpes was nothing compared to what she'd just gone through.

"All right. After lunch tomorrow, boys, we go find our Christmas tree. Now, you mind Leslie and go put together that puzzle. I'm going to the barn to check on some equipment."

As soon as all the Graybows had cleared the kitchen, Leslie collapsed on a chair and breathed deeply. At this rate, she wasn't sure she'd make it to Christmas.

"MOSS! YOU RAT, where are you?" Doug roared as soon as he opened the door to the bunkhouse.

All the men stared at him as if he'd lost his head. Except Moss. He kept his gaze glued to the stick on which he was whittling.

"What's the matter, boss?" Curly asked anxiously.

Doug smiled reassuringly at the timid cowboy. "Nothing that a few words with Moss won't fix. If you don't mind, Moss," he finished with exaggerated politeness.

The others relaxed as Moss stood, a grin on his face. If he wasn't worried, they weren't, either.

"Sure thing, boss. But we can talk out here if you want."

"Don't push it, Moss," he growled in return. His foreman knew he didn't want to discuss Leslie in front of the others. Especially Steve.

Once the door was closed behind them, Doug asked, "What in the hell did you think you were doing?"

"Helping out."

"How?"

"Well, it's this way, Doug. It seemed to me you kind a liked kissin' the lady. I figured a few more opportunities wouldn't hurt. Was I wrong?"

Doug stood there with his hands on his hips, trying to maintain some semblance of anger, but he couldn't. A grin pushed its way across his face. "Nope. You weren't wrong. But don't blame me if Leslie poisons your next piece of pie."

Moss gave a mournful sigh before saying, "For a piece of her pie, it might even be worth it."

Doug shook his head in disgust at Moss's playacting. As he turned to go, the foreman stopped him.

"What are you getting Leslie for Christmas?"

"I don't know. I haven't thought of it. Why? Do you have an idea?"

"Naw. But I think it should be something special. Something to tell her how much we want her to stay."

Moss paused before raising one eyebrow. "I don't suppose you want to consider a diamond ring?"

"Moss, she doesn't want to marry me."

"How do you know?"

Now Doug was thoroughly embarrassed. But Moss was his closest friend, his surrogate father. He'd stood beside him when his parents died, when Bettina was killed, and helped him care for his children. He couldn't lie to him.

"Because I asked her."

"What? When?"

"This morning."

Moss scratched his head. "Just like that? You asked her to marry you at the breakfast table?"

"Not exactly. Last night... Today wasn't the first time I kissed her."

"Uh-huh. And?"

"She said no."

Moss paced across the bunk room and came back to stand in front of him. "Let me get this straight. Last night you kissed her. This morning you proposed. And she said no."

"That's right," Doug replied, exasperated at the dragging out of this topic.

"Did you tell her you love her?"

"Of course not!" After his exclamation, Doug wished he'd kept quiet. He could see Moss wasn't about to.

"Why not?"

"Because I don't!"

"Now don't get all het up. What did you tell her?"

"I said we should get married. Then she'd have a permanent job, and I'd have... what I needed."

"Lord love us, boy, I thought you were smarter than that." Moss shook his head, pity in his gaze.

"Damn it, Moss, I'm not going to lie to her." He turned his back, unable to look his foreman in the eyes.

Moss expelled a huge sigh, then patted him on the back. "No, of course not. Just practice kissing her. Maybe that will do the trick."

LESLIE WAS PREPARED the next time Doug caught her under the mistletoe. She kept a hand between them and brushed his lips lightly with hers before stepping around him.

"Leslie, that wasn't a long kiss," Gareth protested.

"No, it wasn't, sweetie, but I didn't want dinner to burn. You did a nice job setting the table tonight. Didn't they, Doug?"

He was staring at her as if he, too, wanted to protest, but she knew he wouldn't. "Yeah, the table looks nice."

When he agreed with her, she let out the breath she hadn't realized she was holding.

She had them all take their places and served dinner before sitting down with them. Doug said the blessing and then she could relax. Once food was put in front of the Graybow males, a woman could have some peace and quiet.

But a meal only lasted so long.

After the table had been cleared and the dishes done, assisted by all three males, the boys insisted they check the television schedule for another Christmas special. Of course, there was one. Though Leslie had hoped to spend the evening alone, she couldn't disappoint the twins.

However, she did outmaneuver them in the living room. They thought Leslie and Doug should sit in the center of the couch with a twin on either end. Leslie insisted on sitting in the rocker.

She had decided, while working in the kitchen earlier, that she would avoid touching Doug if at all possible. In fact, she'd prefer to avoid being in the same room with him. Her attraction to Doug Graybow was so powerful, she felt as if she were resisting the pull of a giant magnet.

The TV special was a new one about a little boy's visit to Santa. Leslie relaxed, enchanted with the twins' reaction. Sometimes they could look so angelic. Curled up, one on each side of Doug, their gazes glued to the television, they seemed incapable of the mischief they'd created that day.

When the show was over, Justin proved just how unangelic they could be.

"We need to practice, Daddy, so when we visit Santa we'll tell him the right things."

Their father agreed to pretend to be Santa Claus, and Leslie thought hearing what they wanted for Christmas would make her shopping easier.

First Justin, and then Gareth, climbed on Doug's lap and named a puppy as his choice. Justin also asked for the latest action figures he'd seen on television. Gareth added more storybooks and puzzles. Each, before he got down, also whispered something in Santa's ear.

Leslie was sure she knew what they were asking for, but she pretended she didn't. Sometimes, if you ignored children's inappropriate behavior, they would stop. She *thought* that was what she'd read. She certainly hoped so.

"Now it's your turn," Justin said to her, clapping his hands.

She wondered if she'd missed something. Frowning, she looked at Justin. "What's my turn?"

"It's your turn to talk to Santa." He grabbed her hand and tried to pull her from the rocker.

"Don't be silly, Justin. Grown-ups don't talk to Santa."

"Why not?" Gareth asked, coming to stand beside her chair. "Isn't he real?"

She looked at Doug, unable to hide her panic.

"Of course he's real," Doug assured his children.

"Then why don't grown-ups talk to him?" Justin asked.

Leslie answered, fearful of what Doug would say. "Because Santa is for children. He loves them."

"I think he loves you, too, Leslie," Justin said solemnly. "*I* love you."

"I love you, too, sweetheart, but I'm not going to practice talking to Santa."

"But then, how will we know what to get you?" Gareth asked.

"I'll make you a list."

Justin's chin trembled as he protested, "But that's not the same. I want Santa to visit you, too. Please?"

She *knew* she should continue to resist. She knew to do otherwise was insanity. Her gaze met Doug's, and he looked from her to Justin and then back again. She could read his message. For his children.

Getting up from the rocker, she stalked over to Doug. "All right. But we've got to hurry. It's almost your bedtime."

The boys giggled.

"Daddy doesn't have to go to bed early," Gareth explained.

She ignored them and sat down on the couch beside Doug.

"No, Leslie! You have to sit in his lap. Daddy's strong. He can hold you," Justin said.

Oh, yes, he was strong enough to hold her. And to break her heart. She already knew that. Avoiding his gaze, she stood again and gingerly sat down across his knees. One of his arms snaked around her waist and pulled her against him.

"Ho, ho, ho, little girl. Tell Santa what you want for Christmas."

Chapter Fourteen

Doug left his men and headed for the house at about eleven the next morning. He'd decided Leslie shouldn't have to face Mrs. Mablethorpe on her own.

He frowned as he remembered telling Leslie of his decision at breakfast. She hadn't seemed overly impressed with his thoughtfulness. Maybe she was still mad about the Santa Claus thing the night before.

Shifting in the saddle to ease the fit of his suddenly tight jeans, he couldn't stop thinking about how right she'd felt in his arms, her rounded bottom pressed against his thighs. She'd held herself rigid, refusing to lean against him, and she'd stood as soon as she could.

When she took the boys up to bed, he waited for her return. He wasn't sure what he expected, but he wanted to spend more time with her. They could discuss the boys' Christmas, or talk about their childhoods, or— Instead, he'd spent the rest of the evening alone. She'd never come downstairs.

From the barn, as he unsaddled his horse and fed him, he noted two cars parked by the house. One was Mrs. Mablethorpe's, of course, but the other he couldn't quite place. As soon as Diamond was taken care of, he hurried to the house. He'd thought he'd arrive before the guests, but it was clear that he hadn't.

"Leslie?" he called as he entered.

She stepped to the door of the living room, looking beautiful in a blue shirtwaist dress he hadn't seen before. "Doug. I didn't expect you back for a while."

He looked up at the mistletoe, still in place, and then at her lips. Without saying a word, she shook her head slightly and stepped back. "Come join us."

Stepping into the doorway, he automatically greeted Mrs. Mablethorpe and, to his surprise, the Reverend Mr. Shipley and his wife. "I need to go clean up before I can join you. Uh, where are the boys?"

"They're playing in their room until lunch."

"Right. I'll be down in just a minute." He nodded to the other three and then turned and ran up the stairs. Opening the boys' door, he greeted his sons as they worked on a puzzle.

"Hi, guys. Is everything all right?"

"Yeah, Daddy. The pastor and his wife came, too. And that other lady," Justin said.

"Yes, I saw them downstairs. How about Leslie? Is she okay?"

"We think so, but she explained that we shouldn't say anything about mistletoe in front of them. She said you can't kiss her 'cause it would make Mrs. Mablethorpe mad."

Gareth followed his brother's explanation with a question. "Why?"

"Why what?"

"Why would it make Mrs. Mablethorpe mad if you kissed Leslie?"

Doug shifted his weight from one leg to the other as he frantically thought. "Uh, because...because we're not married."

"The people on TV aren't married and they kiss."

"What shows have you two been watching?" he asked, hoping to shift the topic of conversation.

The boys shrugged and stared at him, waiting for an answer.

"Look, I promised Leslie I'd be right down. We'll talk later." If he couldn't avoid it. He headed for the bathroom after grabbing a clean shirt and a pair of sweatpants he could put on over his cast.

When he hobbled back down the stairs, Leslie and their guests were relaxed and laughing. He was surprised, somehow expecting Leslie to be uncomfortable. Bettina had never blended into the community.

"Doug, come sit down," the Reverend Mr. Shipley said, smiling at him. "Join us. We're having a delightful time with Leslie. You are so fortunate to have her fill in for you."

"Thank you. Yes, I am fortunate. I'd like to convince her to stay on. I've been looking for a housekeeper for some time, you know."

Leslie sent him a sharp look before saying, "I don't think that would be a good idea, Doug. After all, it wouldn't be appropriate for me to live here permanently."

"Why not?" he demanded, forgetting his guests.

"Well, really, Doug," Mrs. Mablethorpe said, answering in place of Leslie, "it would be highly inappropriate, the two of you sharing the same roof. What would people say?"

"What are they saying now?" he retorted, glaring at the woman.

"Leslie has explained that as long as you're in a cast, she can outrun you," Mrs. Shipley supplied, smiling. In fact, everyone was smiling except Doug.

He turned to Leslie. "Were you implying that I've been chasing you?"

Leslie stiffened. "It was a joke, Doug."

The reverend leaned over and patted Doug's shoulder. "Relax, son. We're all in agreement."

"About what?"

"Well, Mrs. Mablethorpe asked Violet and me to come with her because she was concerned about...well, about you making the same mistake you made the first time."

Doug said nothing, but he knew what they were talking about: his first marriage. And he hated being the subject of discussion.

"But now that we've met Leslie and talked with her, well, we know you're in safe hands. And I can't blame you for falling for her. She's lovely."

Doug swung around to stare at Leslie, wondering what had been said. Her cheeks were flaming, and she looked as upset as Doug. "Who said I was falling for her?"

"I didn't say any such thing," Leslie protested.

"No, of course she didn't," the pastor continued. "But several of your friends saw you Sunday morning. They thought you made a charming couple. And Dr. Kelsey said—"

"Reverend, would you like more coffee?" Leslie suddenly offered.

Doug looked at her suspiciously.

"Ah. Perhaps you're right. More coffee is an excellent idea." The pastor smiled kindly at Doug and held out his coffee cup to Leslie.

As soon as she set down the coffeepot, Leslie stood. "I'd better check on the lunch."

"I'll help you," Doug said, leaping to his feet. He was going to get to the bottom of the strange conversation.

"I'll manage."

"No, I'll help." He followed her from the room.

"Doug, you can't leave the guests alone," she whispered as they entered the kitchen.

"Oh, yes, I can. What's going on in there?"

"Nothing. We were just having a conversation."

"Then why did you interrupt the reverend?"

She plucked an apron off the back of a chair and tied it around her waist, reminding him of June Cleaver in her nice dress. "I didn't think you'd like what Dr. Kelsey had said. So I thought—"

"You'd keep it a secret from me?"

She whirled to face him. "Why are you making such a big deal about a little gossip? Surely you knew there'd be gossip. That's why Mrs. Mablethorpe wanted to come to lunch."

"I know that," he said, though the idea hadn't really bothered him when he'd first broken his leg. He'd been too desperate. "What did Kelsey say?"

"He told the reverend he thought you were—were fond of me and that it was about time." She walked past him to the stove as if she hadn't dropped a bomb on him.

"I'm no such thing!" he roared.

"I know that," she said as she took a casserole dish from the oven.

He moved to her side. "The time will never come when I'll let myself care that much about a woman. I don't believe in love!"

She turned to look at him, her blue eyes wide with what he thought was pity. "I know."

"Why are you looking at me like that?"

"Like what?"

"As if you feel sorry for me. Just because I don't believe in love doesn't mean I'll be unhappy." When she didn't respond, he rushed on. "I don't have to love you to want you. We could make a marriage on that. You know you want me, too."

She shook her head no. Rage filled him that she would deny the one thing he knew for sure. Without a thought of their guests, or his sons, he grabbed her arms and pulled her against him, his mouth descending to hers. He'd prove she wanted him, as much as he wanted her. He'd prove—how heavenly she felt in his arms.

Leslie knew she'd handled everything the wrong way. The visit had been going well until Doug turned up. He was in a strange mood. But his lips were just as magical as they'd ever been. There was something she needed to do, but she couldn't remember what it was. Her head was filled with Doug, with his touch. She melted against him.

"Well, well, well, I guess Dr. Kelsey was right," the Reverend Mr. Shipley said from the doorway. The two ladies accompanying him giggled.

Leslie came abruptly down to earth when Doug dropped his arms and stepped away from her. Though her cheeks were stinging with heat, she kept her head. After all, it wasn't a sin for two unattached people to kiss. "I guess you're hungry. I think everything is ready." She glanced at Doug, anger filling every inch of his big frame. "Doug, would you call the boys down?"

She thought he was going to ignore her. In fact, she thought he was going to leave and refuse to even eat with their guests. When he finally turned and left the kitchen, she let out her breath.

"Doug's been a little touchy since he broke his leg," she explained to the other three. "He really shouldn't be out riding this soon, but he worries about his men overworking."

"He's a good boy," the reverend said, nodding his head. "Life has dealt him some hard blows, but he's survived."

All she could do was nod. Gesturing to the table, she invited them to take their places while she brought the food to the table.

The awkward silence was broken by the children's arrival, followed by a glowering Doug.

Throughout the meal, the guests talked to the boys, leaving Doug and Leslie to their own thoughts. Justin and Gareth willingly explained about their Christmas plans, telling the trio about the puppy they thought Santa would bring them.

Leslie held her breath, afraid they might remember the other request they'd made. That information would finish off an embarrassing session. But though the boys gave her the occasional strange look, they exhibited perfect behavior.

"But I don't see a Christmas tree," Mrs. Mable-thorpe commented. "Surely you'll have a tree? Your mother always decorated her tree beautifully, Doug."

"Yes, she did."

Fortunately, since Doug didn't seem inclined to expand on his brief comment, the boys described all the ornaments they'd discovered from Christmases past.

"And Daddy's going to buy picture ornaments for our baby pictures, too. Then all three of us will be on the tree," Justin said.

"We wanted Leslie to be on the tree, too, but she said she couldn't 'cause she wasn't part of the family," Gareth added, a sad look on his face.

Leslie sank her teeth into her bottom lip and frantically searched for a change of topic. Before she could speak, Mrs. Mablethorpe, who was seated beside Gareth, patted his shoulder and said, "Perhaps you should ask Santa for Leslie to become part of your family."

Both boys' faces shone with excitement. "Yeah!" they cheered.

"We did," Gareth hurriedly added. "I mean, we told Daddy, but he said he didn't think Santa could do that. Do you think he can?"

As if realizing she might have gone too far, which wouldn't be hard since Doug was glaring at her, Mrs. Mablethorpe said hesitantly, "Well, I don't know. But I think it would be a good thing if he could." She returned Doug's look with a determined one of her own.

"I don't need my life arranged by my neighbors," Doug growled.

"I baked a carrot cake for dessert," Leslie hurriedly said, standing to clear the dinner plates. "I hope you like it."

"I'm sure it will be delightful," the Reverend Mr. Shipley said. "You are a magnificent cook. I hope you'll give Violet your casserole recipe, my dear."

"I'll be glad to," Leslie agreed. "Boys, would you carry the saucers and forks to the table?"

"Leslie," Gareth began as he slid from his chair to help her, "why would you put carrots in a cake?"

"It makes the cake taste good, Gareth. Try it and see if you like it."

The boys looked skeptical but they obeyed.

"She'd make a good mother, too," Mrs. Shipley whispered in loud tones across the table, and Leslie cringed.

She wished the luncheon would end now, before Doug became so enraged, he threw their guests out of the house.

An hour later, Mrs. Mablethorpe and the Shipleys finally departed, full of praise for Leslie and sly grins for Doug. She almost felt sorry for him, but he was being such a grouch, she decided she didn't.

"Are we going to get the tree now?" Justin demanded as soon as the cars pulled away.

Doug turned to look at Leslie. "I'm sure you can fit it into your schedule since you are so perfect."

"Listen here, Doug Graybow. Those were your neighbors, not mine. I didn't do anything to deserve any snide remarks." She wasn't going to put up with his nasty attitude.

To her surprise, he didn't protest. Instead, he gave her a sideways grin that tugged at her heart. "I know. But it was a tough afternoon."

The tension melted inside her and she smiled back.

"Merry Christmas," he responded, his gaze flashing to above her head before he leaned over and gently touched her lips with his.

Oh, yeah. The mistletoe.

The kiss was in such contrast to the heated exchange they'd shared in the kitchen, Leslie was surprised to find it moved her almost as much. It was a sharing of their frustrations, their difficulties . . . and their attraction.

"I hope Moss was right about this mushy stuff," Gareth said as they separated, "'cause it sure is dumb."

"Yeah, I'm never gonna kiss a girl," Justin agreed.

"Good idea," Doug said. "You can waste your kisses on a puppy... if Santa brings you one."

THE BOYS WERE DELIGHTED when their father hitched up two large draft horses to a wagon for the tree-fetching trip. Leslie gingerly patted the horses on their soft noses under the twins' guidance.

"Don't you like horses, Leslie?" Justin asked.

"I think they're pretty, but I haven't been around horses at all."

"You don't know how to ride?" Doug asked as he fastened the harnesses.

"No. I guess it's a good thing I'm not going to live on a ranch." Leslie avoided Doug's eyes.

"I'll teach you," he offered as he finished the other horse's harness.

She didn't bother pointing out that she'd be gone in a couple of weeks. It hurt too much to think about it. But Doug had made his intentions clear. He'd marry her, make love to her, live with her, but he wouldn't love her. And that just wasn't enough.

"Daddy's a good teacher, Leslie," Gareth assured her when she didn't respond. "He taught us last summer. And one day we're going to get our own ponies."

"Good for you," Leslie replied. "Did you bring your gloves, Gareth?" At his nod, she added, "You'd better put them on. Justin?"

"I already have mine on," he assured her.

Doug told the boys to climb in the back of the wagon. When Leslie turned to follow them, he stopped her. "You sit up front with me."

With the two adults up front and the boys standing one on each side of them, holding on to the seat, Doug set the wagon in motion. The snow from Sunday's storm was still on the ground, but it wasn't too deep, and the big horses pulled the wagon easily.

"Will we be able to get the tree in the wagon by ourselves?" Leslie asked.

"I think so, unless you want a huge one," Doug teased.

"Oh, yeah!" Gareth shouted. "Let's get one bigger'n the house. As tall as the sky!"

"Not that big, Gareth, or we couldn't put it inside. You do want Santa to leave your presents in the house, don't you? If he brought you a puppy, it might run away if it was left outside."

"Why would it run away if it loves us?" Justin asked.

Leslie swallowed. She didn't like the direction this conversation was taking. "Once your puppy gets to know you, I'm sure it won't run away. But it will probably be its first time away from its mommy. It might be scared."

"Were you scared the first night you stayed with us?" Gareth asked.

"No, of course not. But I'm an adult," she said, but she couldn't help flashing a panicky look at Doug. He seemed to ignore her as he concentrated on his driving.

"Even if you were, you love us now, so you won't leave us," Justin said, a smile on his face. "Right, Leslie?"

"Not—not until after Christmas." Before Justin could think about what she'd said, she shouted, "Stop!"

Doug pulled on the reins even as he frowned at her. "What is it?"

"There's a perfect tree!" Leslie stood and pointed across the meadow.

"Well, you surprised me," Doug drawled. "I thought we'd have to drive a long way, look at a lot of trees. I've heard women like to look a long time."

"Not me. I know what I like when I see it." She looked away from Doug's smile. Yes, she certainly did. Only, she couldn't have what she wanted.

"Okay. We'll take a closer look. Is that okay with you, guys?" Doug asked his boys.

"Yeah, Daddy. We think that tree is perfect, too," Justin said.

"You'd say a mesquite tree was the perfect one for Christmas if Leslie did," Doug complained, but he was grinning.

After a short drive to the tree Leslie picked, Doug halted the wagon, put feed bags on the horses and took his ax from beneath the seat. "Okay, boys, stand here by the wagon with Leslie. We don't want anyone getting hurt."

Leslie and the boys huddled together, sharing their warmth while they watched Doug attack the trunk of the tree. Even beneath his heavy jacket, his strength was apparent. Leslie thought of those strong arms holding her, as he had in the kitchen, and a shiver ran through her.

"Are you cold, Leslie? Daddy put blankets in the wagon in case we needed them," Justin said, frowning in concern.

"No, I'm fine, Justin. I—I was just thinking."

"About how pretty our tree is going to be?"

"That's right. It's going to be the best Christmas tree I've ever seen." The boys agreed, then turned their attention back to their father's efforts. When the tree eventually toppled to the snowy ground, they let out a cheer.

"Okay, I need some helping hands," Doug called, waving to them. They raced over to him, eager to be a part of the tree fetching.

"Grab a strong branch and pull toward the wagon." After they pulled the tree into the wagon, Leslie shouted, "We did it!"

"You doubted us?" Doug asked with a grin.

"Well, it *is* a big tree."

"Teamwork—that's the way to tackle big jobs."

"Yeah, we helped," Justin said, his little chest sticking out with pride. "Me and Gareth are gettin' big."

"Yes, you are," Leslie agreed with a smile.

"Okay, into the wagon," Doug ordered. Leslie noticed he was studying the sky.

"Is anything wrong?"

"No, but I smell snow in the air, and those clouds are pretty thick. We need to get back to the house."

"Where do we ride?" Gareth asked, studying the wagon. "The tree takes up all the room."

"I guess you'll have to sit in Leslie's lap," Doug said.

"Both of us?" Gareth's eyes were wide. "Do you think she can hold both of us?"

"Of course I can. Come on, let me climb up first. Then your dad can help you." Leslie plopped back down in the wooden bench seat and reached out for the twins. Doug helped first Gareth and then Justin each to sit on a knee, and she held their warm little bodies against her. In seconds, Doug had swung up beside her, after storing the feed bags, and they set off for home.

They hadn't gone far before big snowflakes began to drift lazily down from the thick clouds. Snuggled together, their perfect tree behind them, Leslie decided it didn't get any better than this.

Chapter Fifteen

She'd been wrong.

A lazy evening in the living room, a big fire in the fireplace, the excited chatter of the twins, the decorating of the big tree, all combined for even more perfection than their drive back to the house in the snow.

If she'd tried, Leslie knew she couldn't have dreamed up a more satisfying evening. After dinner, all four of them sat in the living room watching another Christmas special. Each boy crawled in an adult's lap, and Leslie and Doug sat side by side on the sofa. They felt like a family.

A family. That's what she'd been looking for when she set out on her drive to Wyoming. But never in her wildest dreams had she thought her search would be so successful. For at least a little while.

"This is neat," Justin whispered, resting his head against her shoulder. "We're just like a real family."

Leslie's gaze flew to Doug's and then away again. He'd heard his son's words. "It's been a nice day, hasn't it?" she finally said, avoiding any mention of the word *family*. She suspected *that* F word was a lot more unacceptable to Doug than any other.

"Yeah," Gareth replied. "Let's not ever take the tree down."

Doug chuckled. "It will turn brown and all the needles will fall off if we don't. I don't think it would look too good that way. Besides, it's because we only put one up once a year that it seems so special."

"Can we put one up next year, too?" Justin asked, anxious. "Even if—even if Leslie isn't here?"

She hugged the little boy closer to her but said nothing, waiting, as the boys were, for their father's response.

"Of course we can. We'll put up a Christmas tree every year. I promise."

The boys clapped their hands and Leslie smiled at Doug. At least, when she was gone, she could believe that each year the boys would have the magic of Christmas.

It was so tempting to tell Doug yes, she would marry him, take what he was offering. Staying under those circumstances was so much more appealing than going away. But it wouldn't work. Her heart hungered for so much more. She would grow bitter and angry, and Doug would find someone else. Someone younger, happier.

"Time for bed, boys," Doug said, interrupting her depressing thoughts. "You've had a big day."

The boys were so tired, Leslie rose to take them upstairs and discovered Doug intended to come with them.

"Two pairs of hands will get them in bed faster. I'm not sure they'll be able to keep their eyes open much longer."

Doug's assistance did speed up the bedtime routine, but the boys still demanded a story, a habit they'd acquired since Leslie's arrival. She read the story self-consciously because Doug, instead of going downstairs, chose to remain and listen also, sitting on the end of Gareth's bed.

After kissing both boys good-night, she followed Doug, clicked off the light and softly closed the door behind them. Then, after drawing a deep breath, she said, "Good night, Doug."

"No, come back downstairs. We'll finish off the hot chocolate you made."

"I'd rather not. I'm tired," she said, hoping to avoid time alone with him.

He took her arm, foiling any attempt at slipping away. "I know, but just for a little while. I'll clean up after we finish."

He left her little choice unless she wanted to make a scene. Warily she walked down the stairs with him. He escorted her to the sofa, insisting she sit down and he would bring the hot chocolate.

When he returned with two steaming mugs, he joined her as he had earlier. But this time there were no happy little boys to chaperon them. She tried unobtrusively to move away, but his intent gaze stopped her.

"Today was perfect."

"Oh, really? You didn't think so at lunch," she reminded him, hoping to avoid any sentimentality.

He grinned. "I didn't react well to their heavy hinting. It was unexpected. Sorry. But the food was perfect. The reverend was right about your cooking."

"I want you to know that I assured them there was nothing—nothing between us, in spite of what Dr. Kelsey said." She hadn't been able to tell him that earlier.

Smiling, he shook his head. "You shouldn't lie like that to a preacher, Leslie. I think that's against the rules."

"What are you talking about?" she whispered, fear filling her. He was going to force a discussion of their relationship, she knew.

"There *is* something between us. And we both know it, in spite of your denials." He ran his arm along the back of the sofa, only inches from her shoulders, and she began to feel trapped.

"Doug, we've already talked about this," she reminded him, hoping to stop what she knew was to come.

"This? What *this,* Leslie?" His teasing smile, lighting those golden brown eyes, almost made her forget her protest.

"I'm here just until your cast comes off. Remember? We don't want the same things, and so—"

She'd stared at the fire, concentrating on what she needed to say, and never saw his lips lowering to hers until his face came between her and the fire. By then it was too late.

His lips covered hers and his arms encircled her, drawing her to him. Not that she protested. The magic of his touch was more than she could resist. Especially tonight, in the dusky light of the twinkling Christmas tree.

As their kisses deepened, his hand slid beneath the sweater she wore, and he caressed her soft skin. Shivers raced up and down her as she trembled against him. Almost too late she pulled back.

"Doug, we have to stop this."

When she avoided his seeking lips, he turned his interest to her neck, nibbling the soft skin, burying his face in her silky hair. In spite of her words, she slid her fingers through his thick blond hair down to his broad shoulders. Wrapped in his arms, she felt secure against the world.

His lips came back to hers when he felt her protest had passed. Once more their breaths intermingled, their tongues danced, their bodies melted against each other. She couldn't say no to the hunger that had built up in the two of them the past two weeks.

Once more his hands slid beneath her clothing. He caressed her breasts, shoving her bra aside to lower his lips to their hardened tips. She lay back against the sofa, her hands buried in his hair, her body aching for him to fill her. How could one man drive her so quickly over the edge?

He leaned back and reached for the snap of her jeans. Leslie ran her hands down his hard chest, loving the feel of him, even through his sweater. She was so focused on touching him that it wasn't until he began sliding her jeans down her legs that she realized they were going beyond what was safe.

"No," she whispered, sliding downward and trying to catch his hands.

Doug relinquished his hold on her jeans and pulled her against him again, his mouth covering hers in a kiss so demanding, she almost forgot her protest.

Breaking off the kiss, Doug whispered, "Let's go upstairs."

He was scooping her up in his arms, assuming her agreement, when she stopped him.

"No—no, I can't." She had to pull herself together quickly, or it would be too late.

"Les, don't you understand? What we have here is special. It will be enough. We can make it work."

She closed her eyes to hide the pain. He was avoiding saying the one thing she needed to hear. He couldn't say he loved her.

"I will go upstairs, and I'll make love with you, as long as you understand that I'm still leaving." It would break her heart, but she'd have to leave or die a slow death. She found it difficult to meet his gaze, but she did.

He frowned, his movements stilled. "What do you mean?"

"I mean I'll sleep with you, Doug, but I won't stay."

Almost throwing her against the couch, he pulled away. "You mean you'll have casual sex with me? That's all this is to you?"

"Casual sex? No, Doug, this isn't casual sex," she protested. "I don't sleep with just anyone because it feels good," she assured him, her chin rising. "I love you."

He looked away and Leslie felt the tears filling her eyes. Why couldn't she take what he was offering? Why did she have to insist on his love? Her gaze fell on the majestic Christmas tree standing in the corner. A tree filled with ornaments bought and hung with love. The crystal globe reflected the glow of the fire, as if his parents' love still lived on.

That's what she had to have. That kind of love. His love. Without it, their lives could not be intertwined.

"If you love me, then why won't you marry me?" he growled, turning back to stare at her.

"You know why. Because you don't love me. I won't settle for second best. Your mother didn't. Neither did mine. They had husbands who loved them, and I want the same thing."

He looked away.

Time seemed suspended as the two of them sat on the sofa, the fire crackling, the tree sparkling in the soft light. Doug said nothing, staring at the fire. Finally Leslie touched his arm.

"Well, Doug? Do we go upstairs?"

Abruptly he pulled her to him, his mouth taking hers in a kiss that sent her temperature soaring, her senses reeling. Then he released her and stood.

"No, Leslie, we don't go upstairs together. Because once I take you to my bed, I'm not letting you go. If you're going to insist on leaving, when what we have here is so right, then you'll go upstairs alone tonight."

Admittedly, she was surprised. He wanted her. That much was obvious, but he was hardheaded, as always. With a sinking heart and a body that was protesting the withdrawal, Leslie rose, refastened her clothes and walked toward the stairs. As she stood on the first step, she looked longingly at the man standing before the fire, his head bowed.

She felt her heart breaking in two as she realized her dream was shattered. Douglas Graybow would not love her. And she could not stay if he didn't.

Doug heard her pause on the stairs. He pleaded with all his heart for her to call to him, to come back, to agree to marry him.

She went up the stairs.

He called himself all kinds of a fool for refusing what she offered. His body wanted her more than he'd ever wanted any woman. She could stir him to greater heights with one look than even Bettina had done with all her flirting.

But he wasn't going to take her under false pretenses. He wasn't going to profess his love, because he didn't believe in love. Whatever it was. What he and Bettina had shared hadn't done either of them any good.

Except for his boys.

He stared at the Christmas tree. For the first time in almost ten years, this house—his home—was filled with the Christmas spirit. His children were happy, the furniture gleamed with care, the air was filled with happiness.

Why couldn't Leslie see that she was throwing away the best of life? For what? Love? An emotion that was unstable, misleading, fleeting?

The urge to cry, something he hadn't done in a long time, filled him. Banking the fire and pulling shut the screen, he then unplugged the Christmas lights. In the darkness, he drew a deep breath and then trudged up the stairs to his lonely bedroom.

Two weeks until Christmas. Two weeks of pretending he didn't want Leslie with every breath he took. Two weeks of pretending everything was wonderful for his children. Two weeks of misery.

He couldn't wait until Christmas.

THE WEDNESDAY BEFORE Christmas, Doug had an appointment to have his leg examined by Jim Kelsey. Much to his surprise, Leslie volunteered to drive him into town. But she asked that Blackie stay in that day and watch the twins. She had some shopping to do that required secrecy.

Since they had avoided being alone the past week and a half, barely speaking except in the presence of the twins, he found her offer curious.

After escorting the twins to the bunkhouse and Blackie's guardianship, Doug limped back to the house.

From the bottom of the staircase, he called, "Leslie, are you ready?"

"I'll be right down."

She appeared at the top of the stairs and he allowed himself the luxury of watching her until she caught his gaze on her. He spun around and headed for the door. Since their argument the night they decorated the tree, he'd kept his distance. But that didn't keep him from wanting her, from lying awake at night, his body throbbing, as he thought about her.

He couldn't keep his mind from dwelling on her. As a result, he'd given up riding fence. He'd lost his concentration too many times and had cut himself. In fact, he was finding himself fairly useless as his thoughts centered on Leslie and her imminent departure more than on his cows.

Sliding into the passenger seat, he closed the door and fastened his seat belt. When Leslie got in behind the wheel and shut her door, a cloud of the light floral perfume she wore filled the car.

He drew a deep breath and gritted his teeth. It was going to be a long ride to town.

"Thanks for offering to drive me in," he finally said as she put the car in motion.

"No problem."

Glaring at her out of the corner of his eye, he sat silently for several miles. Damn it, it wasn't fair. She didn't seem to be suffering at all. Her blue eyes were as clear and shining as ever, her hair soft and silky, her lips full and— He'd better change his line of thought or he'd embarrass himself.

He cleared his throat. "You have shopping to do?"

"Yes."

She acted as if she were speaking to a stranger, not someone who had held her in his arms, he thought irritably.

"Me, too."

She didn't respond.

"Will you have time to drive me a few places after I see the doc?" He hated having to ask, but Jim had warned him not to drive.

"Of course."

"Thank you very much, Your Highness!" he replied, finally giving in to his pent-up frustration.

She threw him a scalding glance and then returned her attention to the road.

Feeling ashamed of his behavior, Doug stared out the window, resolving not to speak again until they reached Riverside. Not that Leslie would care. She seemed unaware of his existence.

Maybe part of his problem was that he'd taken no interest in a woman until Leslie appeared. He'd start looking around for someone to take her place. Someone who'd take care of his boys, warm his bed, cook, clean . . . and settle for what he offered. Yeah, he'd find someone else. After all, since he didn't love Leslie, she could be easily replaced.

There was a sense of bravado about his thoughts that bothered Doug, as if he himself didn't believe what he was thinking. But he refused to dwell on that idea.

When they reached the hospital, Leslie came in and asked Jim how long the examination would take, then promised to return in an hour to collect Doug.

After she walked away, Jim stared at Doug, one eyebrow raised. "You and the little lady have an argument? I felt a norther blow through here."

"Nope." He wasn't about to discuss his problems with Jim Kelsey. He'd already gotten him in trouble with the pastor and Mrs. Mablethorpe.

"You going to marry her? A Christmas wedding would be nice."

"Mind your own business."

"What's the matter with you, Graybow? You seem in a rotten mood."

"I don't want you spreading any rumors like you did the last time I was here," Doug explained. At Jim's surprise, he elaborated. "The pastor and Mrs. Mablethorpe came to visit. They both believe Leslie and I are in love because of your gossip."

"It wouldn't have anything to do with the two of you kissing in the kitchen instead?" Jim teased as he motioned Doug onto the examining table.

Doug turned beet red. "How did you know about that?"

"It's a small town, Doug. Besides, we all want you to be happy. You're a good man. You deserve someone like Leslie." For once, Jim's face was serious.

Touched in spite of himself, Doug turned away. "Leslie doesn't think so," he mumbled.

"What do you mean? Did she turn you down?"

Doug nodded. "I asked her to marry me, but she said no." There. Jim could feed that fact into the gossip mill. At least he wouldn't be accused of letting Leslie get away without asking.

"Why?"

He glared at the nosy doctor and friend. "The usual reasons, I suppose."

"You mean she doesn't love you?"

Now Doug wished he'd kept his mouth shut. But he couldn't lie. "No. She said she loves me."

"Then what's the problem, man?"

"I won't say I love her." At Jim's exasperated expression, he said, "I can't lie to her. I don't believe in that gushy stuff."

"Man, you are the biggest fool I have ever seen," Jim replied and began pushing the examining table toward the door. "You think you're not in love with her? Your eyes follow her everywhere. You try to keep any other man away from her. When I saw you in church, there was so much love among the four of you, I got misty-eyed just watching you. Don't tell me you don't love that woman."

"Fine!" Doug said between gritted teeth. "I won't tell you anything."

"Lie still," Jim commanded, anger in his voice. He put on the leaded apron and moved behind the X-ray machine. After taking several pictures, he shifted Doug's leg and made several more.

When he finished, he came back to the table. "You're telling me you're going to let Leslie walk away, knowing she loves you? Because you're too much of an idiot to recognize you love her?"

"I want her. That's different."

"Oh? So you only want to sleep with Leslie? You don't care about her? If she were hurt, you wouldn't try to help her?"

"Of course I would. But I'd try to help you, too, in spite of your nosiness, so what does that prove?"

"Not much, since you're not going to have babies with me." Jim stared at him, that eyebrow cocked again.

"I'm not having babies with Leslie, either," Doug protested, but the thought of her carrying his child brought a rush of tenderness that stunned him. Bettina's pregnancy had been difficult because of her constant whining and complaining. Somehow he hadn't comprehended the importance of the resulting births.

But the thought of Leslie having his baby, or, if the boys had their way, *babies,* was earth-shattering. Would she have a safe pregnancy? He'd need to hire more help, of course, so she wouldn't tire herself. Without even realizing it, he grinned, knowing she'd resist any coddling. But he'd insist. After all—

"Doug?"

"What?" he frowned, staring at Jim.

"Where did you go? You had a silly grin on your face and you haven't heard anything I said." Jim watched him, even as a nurse came in, carrying his X rays.

"I—I was thinking."

Jim hung his X rays in front of a lighted panel. "Good news. Your cast can come off today. You've healed sooner than I thought."

"No!" Doug impulsively roared.

Jim stared at him. "No, what?"

"No. I don't want the cast to come off today."

"Why not?"

Because Leslie might leave.

He was afraid he'd said those words aloud, but Jim was still staring at him, a puzzled look on his face. He had some thinking to do, and he needed time. Time he might not have if the cast came off today. Their agreement—his and Leslie's—had been that she would stay until the cast came off.

"It still hurts a little, Jim. I'd just feel more comfortable if we could leave the cast on for another week."

"But it's not necessary."

"Will it hurt anything to leave it on another week?"

"No, but it won't do any good, either."

Jim didn't have any idea how much good it might do.

"Maybe not, but humor me on this one, okay? I'll be in next week and we'll take it off then."

"It's your leg," Jim said, shaking his head. "See Sheila about another appointment."

"Okay."

"And think about what I said about Leslie. She's special." Before Doug could answer, Jim left the room.

Doug dressed and limped to the nurse's desk. He'd known Sheila all his life. She was a couple of years younger than him. They'd gone to school together, the two of them and Larry, her husband.

"Hey, Sheila, I need to make an appointment next week to have my cast removed."

"Sure, Doug." She pushed her blond hair back and smiled at him. After consulting the schedule, she offered several different times. He chose one of them, not much caring exactly when, then was surprised when Sheila covered his hand with hers.

"I bet you'll be glad to get that cast off," she teased, smiling at him.

"Sure. How's Larry?"

Her lips quivered before she gave him a small smile. "I thought you knew. Larry and I have parted company."

"Gee, I'm sorry, Sheila. I didn't know."

"It's all right. I'm better off without him. But, you know," she continued, one finger stroking his hand, "I do get a little lonesome." She blinked her lashes at him and smiled. "Don't you?"

So here was his opportunity to find a substitute for Leslie. A willing woman, attractive, used to ranch life, ready to step in Leslie's shoes.

"Doug? Are you finished?" Leslie called from just inside the door.

Both he and Sheila turned to stare at her, but their reactions were different. Sheila nodded a greeting, her eyes cold. Doug was filled with a warmth that toasted his toes.

"Yeah, I'm finished, Leslie." And he kind of thought he was.

Chapter Sixteen

Leslie told herself she had no right to be jealous of the pretty nurse holding hands with Doug. After all, she'd rejected his marriage proposal.

But the irrational urge to strangle the woman didn't go away.

She forced herself to stand by the door and wait for Doug, unwilling to test her resolve by going closer. He limped toward her, a smile on his lips. Had he made a date with the woman? Something had improved his mood since she'd dropped him off.

"How's your leg?" she asked as they walked to the car.

"Doing fine. The cast can come off soon."

Her heart sank. She didn't have much longer. Even though she believed she'd made the right decision, it hurt so much to even think about leaving.

"Did you finish your shopping?"

"Not yet." She had a long list because she wanted this Christmas to be perfect for everyone, a shining memory that would carry her through the lonely years that would follow.

"Can we go to the Riley Leather Shop?"

"Of course. Where is it?"

"Over by the café." He'd ordered special saddles made for his boys his last trip into town, when Leslie had refused to do his shopping for him.

"Shall I wait in the car?" she asked after parking in front of the store.

"No, come in with me. You may see something you like." He still hadn't bought anything for her for Christmas. Maybe she'd point something out.

"Howdy, Doug," Ash Riley called, as they entered the store. "Guess you're here for your order."

"Yeah, Ash. Are they ready?"

"Sure are. Turned out real good." He ducked behind the counter and hefted first one small saddle and then another on the glass top for Doug's inspection.

"Look, they have their names on them," Leslie exclaimed, pleasure filling her face. It was the first time in ten days she'd looked really happy. Doug drank in her smile, quelling the urge to reach for her. His hands tingled as she ran her fingers over the name of each of the twins, carved into the back of each leather saddle.

"They're fine, Ash," he told the craftsman and took out his billfold to pay. Leslie wandered the store while he took care of business. "See anything you want, Leslie?" he asked.

"No, thank you. Your work is beautiful, Mr. Riley," she added, smiling at the owner.

"I could make you a saddle, too," he offered.

"No, I won't be needing a saddle. I'll be leaving soon." The pleasure left her face and she turned toward the door.

Confusion filled Doug. He didn't want her to leave. But seduction hadn't done the trick. In spite of Jim

Kelsey's words, he couldn't let himself believe he loved her. Maybe he was a coward, but coward or not, he had to find some way to keep Leslie. He couldn't let her go.

THE NEXT FEW DAYS flew by. Leslie spent part of it making stockings for the two boys to hang. She'd found an old sewing machine, owned by Doug's mother, and bought material in town. At night, after the boys went to bed, she would go to her room and work on the stockings and other secrets.

Doug had worked long hours, caused by another storm that had rolled through the valley, bringing more snow. The cows had to be fed each day, as well as kept close to the barn, out of drifts. He came in late, exhausted and hungry. Leslie was preparing dinner for the cowboys and leaving it in the oven for them to dish up. Then she'd return to the house, feed the boys and entertain them until Doug appeared.

In spite of the distance between them, she couldn't keep from worrying about him, providing for him. The boys would sit beside him as he thawed out by the fire in the living room, the Christmas tree lights gleaming, and she'd bring in a tray of warm food.

"I can eat at the table, Leslie. This makes extra work for you," he'd protested one evening.

"The boys like to see you. Everyone's more comfortable in here."

Comfortable. That was the perfect word to describe their days. As long as she didn't think about leaving. The twins, too, tried to forget that she might be leaving.

"Leslie, if Santa brings us a puppy, can he live in the house with us?" Gareth asked again one morning, the

Saturday before Christmas. "Agnes didn't like dogs in the house."

"Well, that depends on your father. I don't think he'll mind...if Santa brings you a puppy."

"But you won't mind?" Gareth persisted.

Leslie bit her lip, anxious to avoid stating the obvious, but there seemed no way around it. "No, I won't mind, but I won't be here much longer, you know. You'll have another housekeeper soon."

"No, we won't," Justin protested fiercely. "Santa's going to bring us you for our mommy."

"Justin, remember, I told you Santa can't bring people. Sometimes you just can't have what you ask for."

"I don't see why not," Gareth said. "You like it here, don't you, Leslie?"

"Of course I do, angel, but—but I can't stay."

"Why not?" Justin asked, his brown eyes, so like his father's, big with emotion. "We'll never be happy again if you go."

"Don't say that, Justin. You will be. Maybe I can write letters to you. Will you write to me?"

"Why can't you stay?" Justin demanded, ignoring her idea.

"I can't explain it, Justin. I wish I could, but I can't."

"Doesn't Daddy want you to stay?" Gareth asked.

Leslie wanted to cry. But she couldn't do that, either. "Yes, he does, but I can't."

"I don't understand," Justin said, his bottom lip quivering. "We all want you to stay. You, too. But you can't."

Was she crazy to leave these two? Was she crazy to demand more than Doug could give her? She wasn't sure he'd ever trust love again. His first marriage hadn't been a happy one. It was so tempting to give in. But a tiny corner of her heart protested. It demanded love before it would be quiet.

Gathering both boys to her, she hugged them tightly. "Please, just be happy. I love you very much. I want this Christmas to be perfect for you. Okay?" She wiped away the tears that slipped from her eyes, and then the boys' tears, too. "We're going to have the best Christmas ever, okay?"

Pressed against her, the two boys nodded, and Gareth sniffed. They remained in each other's arms, locked in the love they shared.

"What's this—a hugathon?" Doug asked from the doorway.

Leslie got up from her knees, surprised, hoping he couldn't tell she'd been crying. "Uh, we were just talking about Christmas," she said and hurriedly turned her back on him. "What are you doing in so early?"

"It's Saturday, and a thaw has set in. We didn't have to haul hay today." He sat down at the table and took a boy on each knee. "Can you spare a cup of coffee?"

"Of course. Boys, would you like to get your daddy some of the candy we made? He might like a snack."

"You made candy?"

"Yeah, we made chocolate candy and white candy," Justin said, bringing his father a plate.

"It all looks terrific. Which is best, chocolate or white?"

Leslie carried him his cup of coffee while the boys debated the candy. When she set down the cup, he caught her hand.

"You've been working hard," he said.

She said nothing, looking away and wriggling her hand free.

"Leslie's making this the best Christmas ever," Justin said, and she smiled at him. He'd wiped his tears away and put on a happy face just for her.

"Indeed she is," Doug agreed. "The best Christmas ever."

Leslie wanted to cry again.

CHRISTMAS EVE.

The boys had worn themselves out with excitement.

The house was filled with fragrant Christmas smells—the fir tree, peppermint candles, sugar and spice.

Presents were wrapped and under the tree. They had gone to town with their father several days ago and come home with packages that they took great care to hide. Doug had even helped them wrap their gifts.

Doug had picked up the puppies earlier in the day and hidden them in the barn. Leslie had made a quick trip down to visit the squirming, yelping babies, just to make sure he'd gotten the right ones. When he brought them to the house tonight after the boys went to bed, she'd tie red bows around their necks.

The turkey was in the refrigerator, waiting to be placed in the oven early in the morning. She'd already prepared several of the dishes to accompany it. Everything was ready for Santa's visit.

Except her heart.

She was so miserable, tears seemed at hand every moment. She realized she had only a few days left, and the pain that thought caused seemed always near. It took so much effort to appear cheerful around the boys, she found herself withdrawing more and more. She could scarcely bear to be in the same room with Doug.

After their argument, he'd avoided her, making everything easier. But the past few days he'd changed his behavior. She'd catch him staring at her, as if he'd never seen her before. He'd touch her hand when she brought him coffee, or put his arm around her shoulder and squeeze gently. She wanted to scream, begging him not to touch her... or to touch her so much more.

She feared she was losing her mind.

If not that, she was certainly losing weight. When she looked in the mirror this morning, she thought she was seeing a ghost. Her face was pale, her cheekbones more prominent. If she didn't leave soon, she'd be skin and bones.

Shrugging her shoulders, she realized it didn't matter. She wasn't going to recover overnight. Misery would be her company for a long time after she left the Bar-G Ranch.

After tucking the boys into bed, Doug at her side, he left to go to the bunkhouse. He wanted to visit with the cowboys, give them their bonuses and then bring the puppies to the house.

Only a couple of minutes after he left, the phone rang.

"Bar-G Ranch," she answered.

"Leslie? This is Jim Kelsey. Merry Christmas."

"Merry Christmas, Dr. Kelsey."

"Is Doug there?"

"He just went down to the bunkhouse."

"Well, never mind. I wanted to wish him Merry Christmas, but you can do that for me. How's his leg?"

"Just fine."

"I still don't understand why he didn't get the cast off the other day. Has he said anything to you?"

Leslie froze. Surely she hadn't understood the doctor's words. "You offered to take off the cast last Wednesday?"

"Yeah. Didn't he tell you? He insisted on keeping it on."

"No, he didn't tell me."

"Well, wish him Merry Christmas anyway. I'll see him next week, and we'll take care of that cast then."

The doctor hung up the phone and Leslie finally did the same. But she didn't move. Raw anger coursed through her. All the agony she'd suffered this past week had been for nothing. Douglas Graybow had tricked her into staying for his convenience, even though her heart was breaking.

How dare he torture her like that!

Without thought, she rushed up the stairs and threw her belongings, considerably more than she'd brought with her, into her bags. What wouldn't fit she hauled down the stairs in her arms, out to her car.

All that filled her mind was anger and pain. She'd stood all she could, waiting for his cast to be removed. And he'd refused.

She finished packing the car and had one last thing to do before leaving—the hardest. She had to say goodbye to the boys. She climbed the stairs to their room one last time and stopped outside the door. Opening it, she tiptoed over to their beds and bent and kissed them each on the cheek. "Goodbye, boys. I love you," she whispered, tears streaming down her cheeks. "I'll miss you both."

After leaving their room, she went to the phone and made a call. "Moss? Can you come to the house?"

When he agreed, she hung up and paced the front hall. She wouldn't leave the children unprotected, but she wouldn't stay a moment longer. When Moss knocked on the door, she opened it and stepped outside.

"What's up, Leslie? Need help playing Santa? Doug should be—"

"Stay with the children until Doug comes back, okay?"

"Sure. Where are you going?"

She almost broke down. But anger sustained her. She stepped close to Moss and kissed his cheek. Then she whispered, "I'm leaving."

Without giving him time to answer, she got in her car and drove away.

MOSS WASTED NO TIME. He ran for the phone and rang the bunkhouse. "Curly, find Doug!"

When Doug, standing beside Curly, took the phone, Moss shouted, "Leslie's gone."

"What? What are you talking about?"

"She told me to come to the house. Then she kissed my cheek and said she was leaving. And she's gone!"

His boss didn't answer. The sound of the phone bouncing off the floor made Moss hold it away from his ear. He heard someone pick it up and then Curly's voice simply said, "He's comin'."

Moss went to the front porch and waited. Doug ran the distance between the two buildings, a puppy under each arm. "What happened?" he gasped as he leapt on the porch.

"I don't know. She just left."

Doug thrust the puppies at Moss and ran for his pickup truck. "Stay with the boys!" he roared over his shoulder.

All Doug could think about as he started the truck and jammed his foot on the accelerator was that he'd waited too long. He'd spent the past few days avoiding facing the truth, hiding from his feelings, playing games with his mind. Did he love Leslie? Or just want her?

This morning he'd gone through his mother's belongings, looking for a present for Leslie. Now, when it might be too late, he knew what to give Leslie for Christmas.

Now, when she'd already left, he knew his feelings.

Finally he knew the truth. Because he realized he couldn't live without Leslie in his life. And if that wasn't love, it would do just as well.

LESLIE HAD ALMOST REACHED the highway when she realized what she was doing. Thinking only of herself and her pain. But two little boys, sleeping innocently in their beds, would have their perfect Christmas ruined if she didn't stop. They wouldn't even know she'd said goodbye. She remembered that day she'd promised she wouldn't leave without saying goodbye. Sneaking out in the middle of the night didn't count.

She lifted her foot from the accelerator as she debated her decision. The thought of facing Doug hurt so much, but the idea of destroying Justin and Gareth's Christmas was even more painful.

Reluctantly, she put her foot on the brake, swung the wheel and turned her car around. She'd go back. But when Christmas was finished, she was leaving. And nothing would make her stay.

As soon as she made her decision, she urged her car to go faster, as fast as she could in the snow now beginning to stick to the road. Through the swirling flakes she saw a pair of headlights dancing in the darkness, coming toward her. As the pickup drove past her, she recognized a wild-eyed Doug staring at her. Her heart fluttered in her throat as she watched in the rearview mirror when he slung the truck around, its tires screeching, to come after her. He looked furious. Well, he could just be angry. She was angry, too.

He caught up to her, but made no attempt to pass her. Following her as if he were a sheepherder bringing her home, he drove right behind her, his lights reflecting in her rearview mirror.

When she came to a stop and turned off the motor, Doug was at her door before she could open it.

"What in the hell do you think you were doing?" he demanded, rage on his face.

"I was leaving," she said as she stepped out of the car. There was no point in trying to hide it since he could see her bags.

She expected questions or his ranting and raving. Lifting her chin, she waited for his anger to rain down on her. Instead, he seized her arms and pulled her against him, his mouth taking hers as she opened it to protest.

He kissed her like a man starving for love. He kissed her as if she were a well of water and he was a man dying of thirst. He kissed her as if he'd never let her go.

But he would. He had. He didn't love her. In spite of his touch, his kisses, tears slid out of the corners of her eyes. He was only prolonging the agony.

Doug didn't feel her tears at first. He was so overcome with the realization that he loved this woman, he wasn't even aware of the cold. But one lone tear strayed into their kiss, and he tasted the salt of her crying.

"Leslie?" he whispered, drawing away only an inch or two. "Don't cry, baby, please don't cry. Did I hurt you?"

She shook her head and buried her face in his chest.

"Why are you crying?" he asked gently, lifting her chin so he could see her. She kept her eyes closed and tears streamed down her pale face.

"It hurts too much, Doug. I can't—I can't keep saying goodbye," she finally sobbed and twisted her chin from his hold. Again she burrowed into his chest.

Staring up at the dark sky, filled with stars, he said a silent prayer of thanks for his awakening. Then he lowered his lips to her cold cheek. "Leslie? Baby, look up at the stars. Do you see them?"

She shook her head no.

"Look up, sweetheart. I want you to see those stars. It's Christmas Eve and they're pretty special."

He grinned as she finally raised her face, growing irritation laced with her tears. "I know it's Christmas Eve. That's why I came back, you ignoramus!"

"Now that's not a nice thing to call your husband, my love," he teased, exhilaration filling him.

"Don't tease me," she muttered, pushing against his chest.

The silly woman thought she was going to leave his arms. "No, sweetheart, I won't tease you. But by those stars shining in the sky, I promise to love you for the rest of my life.''

She grew very still, pressed against his heart, and he waited with all the anticipation his children would feel in the morning when they crept down the stairs.

''What—what did you say?''

''Look at me, Leslie.'' He waited until this time her blue eyes peeped up at him. ''I said I love you—and will always love you.''

''Doug? You mean it? You're not—not just telling me that so I'll stay?'' Her voice trembled as well as her body and he held her close.

''I mean it,'' he whispered in her ear as he gathered her even closer.

''When did you decide? I mean, I've been waiting so long. I can't—''

''Sweetheart, I wish I could say I knew right away. I've wasted so much time,'' he said, pressing kisses all over her face. ''My body's been telling me for a long time. My heart's been trying to tell me. But I was so scared. I didn't know for sure until Moss said you'd left.''

''I didn't want to go,'' she assured him, kissing him in return. When their lips touched, several minutes passed before he could continue his explanation.

''That's when I knew that you were the most important thing in my world. I can't live without you, Leslie. Don't ever leave me.''

''No, never,'' she breathed into his mouth just before his lips met hers.

''You folks comin' inside or what?'' Moss called from the front porch.

They broke apart and Doug's heart sang as Leslie giggled. How he loved her laughter. Without a word, he scooped her into his arms and carried her to the door.

"You be careful, now. You don't want to break another leg," Moss warned, holding the two puppies and watching them.

"You're right, I don't. Moss, take those pups back to the bunkhouse. I'll come get them in the morning."

"Right. Welcome home, Leslie," the cowboy added as he started down the steps.

Doug waited until Moss was out of the circle of light from the porch before he turned to the door, repeating Moss's words. "Welcome home, Leslie."

Once inside, he continued right up the stairs. "Will you stay with me tonight, Les? I don't want to wait any longer. But I will, if that's what you want."

More tears filled her eyes as she beamed up at him. "No, I want to be with you, Doug. Tonight and forever."

This time, when they fell across Doug's big bed, there was no interruption, no anger and no misunderstandings. Leslie unbuttoned his shirt as he helped her with the same task. Jeans fell to the floor after a tug of war with his cast and cowboy boot.

"Damn, when this cast comes off, I'm going to have to start wearing sneakers," Doug teased as the boot finally came off.

"I don't think I can see you in sneakers, cowboy." She laughed. "You're still wearing too many clothes," she teased, sliding her hands over the band of his underwear.

"So what's stopping you from taking care of that?" he asked as he himself worked on removing her bra. She didn't waste time answering.

As warm flesh pressed against warm flesh, lips joined and their bodies became one, Leslie rejoiced because their hearts were also one. She couldn't have asked for a nicer Christmas present.

"DADDY! DADDY! Leslie's gone!" Justin yelled, pounding on his father's bedroom door.

Hoping it was time to go downstairs and see what Santa had brought them, the boys had knocked on Leslie's door. When she hadn't answered, they'd opened it and tiptoed in.

Finding a neatly made bed and a room empty of Leslie's belongings, they'd run to their father's room. It was unusual to find the door locked, but that didn't calm their fears.

"Daddy!" Gareth seconded. "Come quick. We've got to find Leslie!"

"Boys, calm down. It's okay," their father called.

"Daddy, you don't understand," Justin pleaded, tears falling. "Leslie's gone. We love her so much, we thought Santa would make her our mommy, but she's gone."

"No, I'm not!" Leslie called.

Both boys' eyes widened and they stared at each other.

"Leslie?" Justin called cautiously.

"Yes, it's me. I'll—I'll be right there."

"What are you doing in Daddy's room?"

There was no answer, just a rustling sound. Then the door swung open and their father blocked the doorway. "Look, guys, Leslie and I have a surprise for you, but, uh, she needs a couple of minutes, okay? Why don't you go wait by the tree?"

"She's going to be our mommy, isn't she?" Justin demanded, not fooled by his father's stalling tactics.

"Yea!" Gareth shouted, jumping up and down. "Leslie's going to be our mommy! Thank you, Santa!"

The sound of someone knocking on the front door surprised all three Graybows. Then Doug said, "I bet that's Moss with a delivery from Santa. Go let him in, boys, okay?"

Grinning, the boys scrambled down the stairs and swung open the door. They were surprised to discover Mrs. Mablethorpe, the Reverend Mr. Shipley and his wife.

"Good morning," the preacher said, a big smile on his face. "We thought you'd be up early. We're dropping by to wish you a Merry Christmas."

His wife held out a basket with baked goods and Mrs. Mablethorpe held a pot with a poinsettia in it. Justin looked at Gareth and then said, "Thank you. Merry Christmas."

"Has Santa been good to you?" Mrs. Mablethorpe asked, bending toward them.

Gareth couldn't keep silent. "Yeah! He brought us Leslie for a mommy!"

"Who is it?" Doug called out as he and Leslie came down the stairs behind them. "Moss?" The boys parted and Doug saw the pastor.

"My, my, my," the Reverend Mr. Shipley murmured, a shocked look on his face as he saw a shirtless Doug in a pair of ski pants and Leslie in a man's blanket robe. "Ladies," he said to his companions, "I think we've come just in time to complete Santa's gift. I hope a ceremony is in your plans?'' he added, addressing Doug.

Doug looked down at the beautiful woman beside him, his heart full of love, and kissed her on the lips. Then he lifted her left hand, bearing his mother's ring, and showed it to his guests.

"Oh, yes, we're going to have a ceremony. In fact, I'll have one every day if necessary."

With a laugh in spite of her flushed cheeks, Leslie said, "I think one will be sufficient, if you don't mind, Reverend. A Christmas wedding will be perfect."

Epilogue

"Doug?"

Leslie's whispered call just barely reached Doug as he knelt beneath the Christmas tree. He was putting together a train set Justin and Gareth had requested for Christmas.

"Yeah, honey?" he called softly. She'd gone to the kitchen to make them both a cup of hot chocolate.

"Doug, it's time."

She must be tired. She should be. As always, she'd outdone herself preparing for Christmas. Justin and Gareth expected it to be the most important holiday of the year now. Sam and Steven just knew their mommy was making them lots of cookies and candy. Two years old, they liked the idea of presents, but not waiting.

"I'm almost through, Les," he called back. Tomorrow, after Christmas dinner, he intended for her to go to bed and stay for a while. With the baby due next week, she'd been on her feet too much.

"No, Doug, I mean it's time," she said, from the doorway.

He whirled around, almost falling over. Something in the way she said the words this time told him she wasn't talking about Christmas.

Leaping to his feet, he rushed to her side. "You mean you've gone into labor? Now? But it's early. You can't—"

A pain seized her and he eased her over to the sofa. "Honey, wait here. I'll get your bag and call Jim."

"There's no time," she whispered, and he froze.

"What do you mean?"

"Doug, the pains are about a minute apart. Call Jim, but I'm afraid you're going to have to deliver this baby on your own."

"Oh, no," he moaned and raced for the phone. He'd delivered baby calves, but never a child. When Jim answered the phone, he assured Doug he could manage, and Jim and an ambulance would be there as soon as possible.

Doug came back into the living room, his hands shaking. "Sweetheart, Jim's on his way, but I'll do the best I can."

She smiled at him, a smile that he'd never grow tired of seeing. "You'll take care of us. You always have."

"Let's get you upstairs—" he began, when another pain seized her.

"I—I think this baby wants to be born by the Christmas tree," she gasped. "Now!"

WHEN JIM ARRIVED at ten to one in the morning, he discovered mother and daughter lying on the sofa in the living room, the Christmas tree lights sparkling brightly.

"Everyone okay?" he asked a beaming Doug.

"Everyone's terrific. Santa just came a little early, that's all."

"How about you, Les? Any problems?"

"No," she said with a soft chuckle as she nuzzled her baby's head. "Having one is a lot easier than twins."

"So I've heard," the doctor agreed with a smile.

After checking out his patients, Jim turned to Doug. "You guys have a thing about Christmas, don't you?"

Doug grinned. His second set of twins had been conceived that Christmas three years ago when Leslie had first come into his life. Now their third child had chosen to appear shortly after midnight on Christmas Day. The boys were going to have a real surprise in the morning. A sister, finally.

"I guess it's our lucky day," he replied, taking Leslie's hand in his. "And this year, we've been given a little angel." He bent over to kiss first Leslie and then the sleeping baby. "Yeah, our lucky day," he repeated as he and Leslie exchanged smiles by the twinkling lights of the Christmas tree.

**UNLOCK THE DOOR TO GREAT ROMANCE
AT BRIDE'S BAY RESORT**

Join Harlequin's new across-the-lines series, set
in an exclusive hotel on an island off the coast of
South Carolina.

Seven of your favorite authors will bring you exciting stories
about fascinating heroes and heroines discovering love at
Bride's Bay Resort.

Look for these fabulous stories coming to a store near you
beginning in January 1996.

Harlequin American Romance #613 in January
Matchmaking Baby by Cathy Gillen Thacker

Harlequin Presents #1794 in February
Indiscretions by Robyn Donald

Harlequin Intrigue #362 in March
Love and Lies by Dawn Stewardson

Harlequin Romance #3404 in April
Make Believe Engagement by Day Leclaire

Harlequin Temptation #588 in May
Stranger in the Night by Roseanne Williams

Harlequin Superromance #695 in June
Married to a Stranger by Connie Bennett

Harlequin Historicals #324 in July
Dulcie's Gift by Ruth Langan

Visit Bride's Bay Resort each month wherever
Harlequin books are sold.

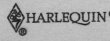

HARLEQUIN ®

BBAYG

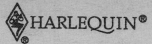

HARLEQUIN®

Don't miss these Harlequin favorites by some of our most distinguished authors!
And now you can receive a discount by ordering two or more titles!

HT#25593	WHAT MIGHT HAVE BEEN by Glenda Sanders	$2.99 U.S. ☐ /$3.50 CAN. ☐
HP#11713	AN UNSUITABLE WIFE by Lindsay Armstrong	$2.99 U.S. ☐ /$3.50 CAN. ☐
HR#03356	BACHELOR'S FAMILY by Jessica Steele	$2.99 U.S.☐ /$3.50 CAN. ☐
HS#70494	THE BIG SECRET by Janice Kaiser	$3.39 ☐
HI#22196	CHILD'S PLAY by Bethany Campbell	$2.89 ☐
HAR#16553	THE MARRYING TYPE by Judith Arnold	$3.50 U.S. ☐ /$3.99 CAN. ☐
HH#28844	THE TEMPTING OF JULIA by Maura Seger	$3.99 U.S ☐ /$4.50 CAN. ☐

(limited quantities available on certain titles)

AMOUNT	$
DEDUCT: 10% DISCOUNT FOR 2+ BOOKS	$
POSTAGE & HANDLING ($1.00 for one book, 50¢ for each additional)	$
APPLICABLE TAXES*	$_____
TOTAL PAYABLE	$_____

(check or money order—please do not send cash)

To order, complete this form and send it, along with a check or money order for the total above, payable to Harlequin Books, to: **In the U.S.:** 3010 Walden Avenue, P.O. Box 9047, Buffalo, NY 14269-9047; **In Canada:** P.O. Box 613, Fort Erie, Ontario, L2A 5X3.

Name: _____

Address: _____ City: _____

State/Prov.: _____ Zip/Postal Code: _____

*New York residents remit applicable sales taxes.
Canadian residents remit applicable GST and provincial taxes.

HBACK-OD2

HARLEQUIN®

A M E R I C A N ◆ R O M A N C E®

"Whether you want him for business...or pleasure, for one month or for one night, we have the husband you've been looking for. When circumstances dictate the need for the appearance of a man in your life, call 1-800-HUSBAND for an uncomplicated, uncompromising solution. Call now.
Operators are standing by...."

Pick up the phone—along with five desperate singles—and enter the Harrington Agency, where no one lacks a perfect mate. Only thing is, there's no guarantee this will stay a business arrangement....

For five fun-filled frolics with the mate of your dreams, catch all the 1-800-HUSBAND books:

Coming to you only from American Romance!

HARLEQUIN®

A M E R I C A N ◆ R O M A N C E®

You asked for it...You got it! More MEN!

MORE THAN MEN

We're thrilled to bring you another special edition of the popular MORE THAN MEN series.

Like those who have come before him, Connor O'Flaherty is more than tall, dark and handsome. All of those men have extraordinary powers that make them "more than men." But whether they are able to grant you three wishes, or live forever, make no mistake—their greatest, most extraordinary power is of seduction.

So make a date with Connor O'Flaherty in...

> #614 A LITTLE SOMETHING EXTRA
> by Pam McCutcheon
> January 1996

MTM5

Harlequin Romance ®

brings you

Some men are worth waiting for!

Beginning in January, Harlequin Romance will be bringing you some of the world's most eligible men. They're handsome, they're charming, but, best of all, they're single! Twelve lucky women are about to discover that finding Mr. Right is not a problem—it's holding on to him!

In the coming months, watch for our Holding Out for a Hero flash on books by some of your favorite authors, including LEIGH MICHAELS, JEANNE ALLAN, BETTY NEELS, LUCY GORDON and REBECCA WINTERS!

INTRODUCING...  **WINNERS CIRCLE**

A collection of award-winning books by award-winning authors! From Harlequin and Silhouette.

Falling Angel
by Anne Stuart

WINNER OF THE RITA AWARD
FOR BEST ROMANCE!

Falling Angel by Anne Stuart is a RITA Award winner, voted Best Romance. A truly wonderful story, *Falling Angel* will transport you into a world of hidden identities, second chances and the magic of falling in love.

"Ms. Stuart's talent shines like the brightest of stars, making it very obvious that her ultimate destiny is to be the next romance author at the top of the best-seller charts."
—*Affaire de Coeur*

A heartwarming story for the holidays. You won't want to miss award-winning *Falling Angel*, available this January wherever Harlequin and Silhouette books are sold.

Harlequin Romance ®

brings you

How the West Was Wooed!

Harlequin Romance would like to welcome you Back to the Ranch again in 1996 with our new miniseries, Hitched! We've rounded up twelve of our most popular authors, and the result is a whole year of romance, Western-style. Every month we'll be bringing you a spirited, independent woman whose heart is about to be lassoed by a rugged, handsome, one-hundred-percent cowboy!

Watch for books branded Hitched! in the coming months. We'll be featuring all your favorite writers including, Patricia Knoll, Ruth Jean Dale, Rebecca Winters and Patricia Wilson, to mention a few!

HITCH-G